Captivating Captains

THE CAPTAIN
AND
THE BEST MAN

CATHERINE CURZON &
ELEANOR HARKSTEAD

The Captain and the Best Man
ISBN # 978-1-83943-830-1
©Copyright Catherine Curzon and Eleanor Harkstead 2019
Cover Art by Cherith Vaughan ©Copyright December 2019
Interior text design by Claire Siemaszkiewicz
Pride Publishing

THE CAPTAIN
AND
THE BEST MAN

Dedication

CC – To all the pilots that wave.
EH – For my mum.

Chapter One

The farthest Josh had ever traveled before was Magaluf. He glanced at his boarding pass again as he headed to the departure lounge, still not quite believing what it said.

Pointe-à-Pitre, Guadeloupe.

Nine hours on a plane.

At least I can have a nap.

Josh trundled his cabin bag through Duty Free and left with aftershave and sunglasses that he wasn't sure he needed. Then he found a café, the perfect place to camp out with a book and kill time before the flight. Half-asleep, Josh clambered over other people's luggage to join the queue.

Nine hours in steerage.

The cafe's prices seemed only slightly more reasonable than the eye-watering first-class ticket that Josh couldn't afford, but he could treat himself at least. An array of elaborate, decadent pastries filled the glass-fronted cabinet, tempting any travelers who were about to submit to airline food, and Josh was happy to surrender to their charms. It was a nice way to start the holiday, after all.

Where are all these people going? he wondered idly as he waited to be served. Screaming babies, excited gaggles of students with packs on their backs, stressed-looking business types and children zooming around making plane noises, all of them ready to escape the autumn drizzle.

Josh ordered a latte, then selected a cinnamon bun from the pastries on offer. It was the last one, a complicated twist of pastry zigzagged with icing and dark with cinnamon. He'd never seen a bun like it.

"If that's *really* the last bun, you'd better hope you're not on *my* flight," a plummy voice announced from behind Josh. "Or I'll make it a bumpy landing."

"It's the last one," the young woman who was serving Josh said with a comical pout, a red flush creeping over her throat. "Sorry, Cap!"

Cap?

When Josh turned to face the man behind him, his fringe swished into his eyes. He brushed it away with the back of his hand as he looked up.

Bloody hell.

There behind him in the queue was a pilot clad in the sort of immaculate uniform he could only have dreamed of—every button shiny, every seam straight, his hat at a perfect angle on his head. But Josh barely noticed because his gaze was drawn to the pilot's handsome, chiseled face.

"I...erm...sorry! I don't mind having an almond croissant instead, if you've got your heart set on a cinnamon bun."

"Well it *is* my birthday," the pilot told him, his expression somber. Then he blinked his blue eyes and smiled. "But I'm a nice fellow, so take it. It's my treat." He looked to the woman behind the counter, who was beaming at him, Josh entirely forgotten in the wake of the *Cap*. "Throw me something nice with pistachios into a bag and a *huge* cup of tea, please! I'm paying for His Cinnamon Munching Majesty here, too. And something for you as well, of course! Happy birthday to me, eh?"

Josh smiled. A stranger — *a pilot, no less* — was footing his bill. "You really don't have to!"

The bright lights of the café picked out discreet flecks of silver in the pilot's hair and Josh couldn't look away. The man was so effortlessly confident and self-assured. *Radiant.* And at this time of the morning, too. "But…if you insist. And — happy birthday, by the way."

"Thirty again." The pilot grinned. "I've been thirty for about nineteen years now, but don't tell anyone."

"Do you keep a portrait in your attic or something? You're never — " *Forty-nine?* Josh stopped himself before he announced the man's age across the café. "I'm thirty next year," Josh volunteered, though he had no idea why.

"Happy early thirtieth." He chuckled, handing a note to the woman. "Take my advice and always claim to be thirty next birthday. It's a good age to be, even for nineteen years."

Josh chuckled. "And what if I claim to be twenty-nine again next year? Then I'll always be a year younger than you!"

Always? Josh glanced away. *You don't say always to the man stood behind you in the queue, who's about to fly off to God knows where.* Josh looked instead at the bottles of syrup along the shelf and caught the pilot's reflection in the mirrored wall behind.

What a smile.

"It's a deal," was the reply. "Maturity is *vastly* overrated, after all."

"Oh, I don't know about that." Josh turned back to the pilot with a grin. *Why not?* If he was straight, the bloke wouldn't notice he was flirting. "Maturity can be *very* nice indeed."

He heard the tinkle of coins as the pilot dropped his change into the tip cup. "Well, this birthday's getting better. No cinnamon bun this morning, but you've more than made up for it."

They stood at the end of the counter, waiting for their drinks.

"Is it your favorite?" Josh asked. "I honestly don't mind relinquishing it. Seeing as it's your birthday. That bun does look amazing, but so do all the others."

"I wouldn't dream of it!" The pilot nodded toward a brightly decorated paper bag on the counter. "Whatever's in there will be just as tasty. Besides, I can always have something special when you and I go out to dinner. If you'd let an old reprobate like me take you to dinner, that is?"

Stunned, Josh rubbed his tired eyes and blinked. "I'm not imagining things, am I? You did just invite me to dinner?"

"Don't tell me you're flying out of Blighty for good?" The pilot's grin grew more mischievous. "I'm off on a bit of a jolly once I clock off but I'm safely back on British shores in a fortnight. What do you say?"

"I'd say very definitely *yes*. I'm going to my friend's wedding, but I'll be back in a week. So…once you've returned from your *jolly*, let's meet." Josh's face began to ache from smiling. He added, "I'm Josh, by the way."

"Guy," he replied. *Guy.* How well the name suited him. *Guy the pilot. Guy with the immaculate uniform and blue eyes. Happy birthday to Guy.* "Hello, Josh!"

Not knowing what else to do, Josh held out his hand to shake. "Hello, Guy."

Gorgeous Guy.

Who was about to hop into the cockpit and fly off who knew where.

Guy took Josh's hand in his own and shook it. Josh was barely aware of the drinks arriving, his placed on the tray with a clink of crockery, Guy's in a takeaway cup. When Guy released Josh's hand, he reached into the well-cut jacket of his uniform and took out a silver pen.

A fountain pen, Josh noted. *Just right.*

"Let me give you my number," Guy said. Josh resisted the urge to tell him he could put it straight into his phone, because there was something about that dark blue ink and the swirl of handwriting as Guy wrote on one of the napkins, something wonderfully traditional. Romantic, even. "There you go!"

"Thanks." Josh carefully laid the napkin on his tray. "Enjoy your flight. And your *jolly*, Captain Guy."

"Enjoy the wedding." Guy gave a little bow. "And *my* cinnamon bun."

"I intend to!" Josh said. "We'll speak soon."

With another flash of that brilliant smile Guy picked up the cup. He raised his cap momentarily to Josh, then picked up the bag and said, "Happy flying!"

"Bye!" Josh waved.

Why did they both have to go their separate ways so soon after meeting? But Josh had Captain Guy's number. They'd meet again, he knew it.

He watched Guy stride away across the wide expanse of gleaming floor. He wasn't the only person watching, Josh knew, but he was the one with Guy's number.

Dinner. How could I say no to that?

In a daze—partly brought on by an early start, but mainly due to the last few minutes of his life—Josh took a seat at a table. He put down his tray and tore a piece from his bun. It really was delicious, the pastry melting on his tongue and the—

His table jolted as a little boy in a striped T-shirt accidentally barreled into it.

"You okay?" Josh asked, but the child ran off. Josh shrugged and went back to his bun, only to discover that the child's impact with his table had sent his coffee sloshing over the side of the cup.

And it had saturated the napkin.

Guy's phone number, written with such crisp elegance in fountain pen, was nothing now but a smudged, smeary watercolor. Josh carefully peeled the napkin off the tray and stared at it, trying to decipher the blurred mess. He could just about see a seven... It definitely started with a zero. And there was a three...or was it an eight?...at the end.

The number had gone. Lost. Just as suddenly as Captain Guy had entered Josh's life, he had left it.

Oh, well.

It had been a nice little fantasy while it had lasted. The HR manager and the airline pilot. And now a fantasy was all it'd ever be.

Chapter Two

Josh bought himself more aftershave and shower gel to match it, and nearly bought another pair of sunglasses, but finally his flight was called.

He shuffled into line at the gate with all the other passengers. They were happy, and Josh tried his best to be, but he couldn't help but be haunted by what had slipped through his hands. That voice. Those eyes. And bloody hell, Guy had looked sexy as anything in that uniform.

Worst of all, Guy would just think Josh hadn't bothered, that he was being polite, humoring a bit of flirtation from a charming older man. He'd be waiting for a call that never came and Josh would never be able to explain why.

The thought followed him along the tunnel and onto the aircraft, past the smiling attendants and into the world's smallest, tightest seat.

Nine hours.

Nine hours of thinking about not thinking about Guy and a seat that seems to have been designed for a very small child.

"Mr. Robertson?" An immaculate flight attendant was beside his seat, her coral-pink lips set into a polite smile.

What now?

"Oh—should I put my Duty Free under the seat? It's in the overhead locker, but I can move it, it's okay."

"Your seat's been upgraded to first class, Mr. Robertson," she told him. "Complimentary, of course. Would you follow me, sir?"

Josh started to unfold himself from his seat, but paused. This was crazy. "I'm *Josh* Robertson, yeah? Are you sure you've got the right bloke?"

"There's no mistake," she said with an efficient, cheery politeness. "Of course, if you'd prefer *this* seat, you're welcome to stay here. Would you prefer this seat, sir?"

Josh shot up out of his seat and hit his head on the panel above his head. The air-nozzle went off with a *whoosh.*

"Oooof! No...no, I'd very much like to travel first, thanks!" Josh glanced at her name badge. "Erm...Teri. Thanks."

He was going to be one of the people who turned left. Not right, not into that vast, cramped cabin, but left through the curtain. He was going into Narnia, taking the aisle to the promised land. Every eye seemed to be on Josh as he followed the attendant, past the door and through that mythical curtain.

First class.

Once he passed through the curtain, the very air seemed to change. It felt calmer. Less cramped. Less busy. Spacious, even. And no one yelling for crayons and a coloring book either. Although Josh might have done had he remained squashed into his tiny seat.

Now, though, he had ahead of him only nine hours of luxury.

His seat wasn't so much a seat as a small, self-contained room. A little pod, almost. *His* pod, until Guadeloupe.

"Can I offer you a glass of complimentary champagne?" his fairy godmother asked.

"Is that allowed at ten in the morning?" Josh asked as he settled into his seat. "Because I wouldn't say no." He felt like he'd won the lottery, because clearly he had — they must've wanted to fill a seat in first and drawn a passenger name at random. There was no other way that he could've escaped steerage.

And as if by magic, there it was, bubbles rising gently to the surface.

"Enjoy your flight." The attendant beamed. "Call if you need anything."

"Will do — and thanks!"

Josh set about exploring his new world. A menu — an *actual* menu — three different kinds of champagne to choose from, a beautiful, soft blanket, complimentary earphones which didn't look like they came from Poundland and, more than anything, *space*. Glorious, wonderful, amazing space. Josh stretched his legs out and they didn't meet the seat in front. What a novelty this was. And how completely unexpected.

In fact, he couldn't even *see* the seat in front.

This was how to travel.

Overhead, a speaker buzzed into action and Josh took a sip from his glass, already quite used to this new way of life.

"Ladies and gentlemen, this is your captain speaking. Welcome aboard what I hope will be a very comfortable British Airways flight to Pointe-à-Pitre, Guadeloupe."

Josh glanced up at the speaker above his seat. That sounded a lot like Guy. Pilots always spoke in that smooth, buttery way.

Oh, Guy... The one who got away.

Although Josh still had the soggy napkin wrapped protectively in another napkin in his bag.

"It's lovely to have you with us and you'll be pleased to hear that the doors are closed, the tank's full and it's my birthday. Our marvelous cabin crew will demonstrate safety procedures aboard this triple seven — one of my favorites — and please do go easy on them. They've got a party to go to later."

Josh's hand shook and he unsteadily put his glass down on the table. Birthday? A party? And that little quip about it being his favorite plane?

It's Guy. Guy's flying the bloody plane.

"In nine short hours we'll be landing in Pointe-à-Pitre at three p.m. local time and the forecast is a gloriously sunny one. So sit back, relax and enjoy your flight."

Relax?

Josh had to try very hard not to bound from his seat with glee. Maybe he could ask the flight attendant to take a note to the cockpit for him. Maybe he could —

Surely this was how he'd ended up in first?

It has to be.

Guy must've seen Josh boarding and done whatever it is pilots did to move someone into the best seats in the house. *A second chance!*

And a second chance complete with free champagne!

Josh rummaged in his bag for a pen. Then the thought occurred to him that, as he was now in first, he could probably just ask for a pen and paper without having to send Guy a note scribbled on the back of an old bus ticket. He'd wait until they were in the air, and the next time one of the helpful attendants came by, he'd ask.

Everything seemed so much smoother in first class, from the taxi to the take-off and everything else besides. The cabin was quiet and calm, what Josh imagined it must have been like to fly fifty years ago. It all seemed so glamorous from here, especially with Captain Guy on the flight deck.

If only I'd paid more attention to his hands.

Because then Josh could've imagined him holding the controls. All those lights and buttons and goodness knows what else, and Guy was master of them all. A shiver of delight ran through Josh. Guy wasn't lost to him.

He pulled the blanket up and snuggled comfortably. He'd just have a little nap. After all, he'd gotten up early, and the champagne and travel sickness pill had counteracted the effects of his latte. Although that said, not much had been left in his cup after it had been spilled.

A lovely little nap, in first…then he'd write Guy a note and ask him for his number again…

* * * *

When Josh opened his eyes, he had the feeling that he'd been asleep for some time, but it was hard to know. He blinked at the map on the screen in front of him, showing the plane's progress. They must've been in the air for ages. His mouth felt dry and he reached for his champagne. It wasn't all that cool now, but…there was a piece of folded paper underneath it.

Guy?

Josh unfolded the paper and there, in that same immaculate handwriting, was a short note.

How's my driving? G. x

Josh started to laugh, but clamped his hand over his mouth, keen not to annoy the other passengers by destroying the peace of first class.

And a kiss, too. Josh pressed the note to his lips like a lovestruck teen. Then he hit the button for the flight attendant and waited. She was beside him in what seemed like seconds, still perfect, still smiling.

"Sir?"

"Could I possibly trouble you for some writing paper and a pen, please?" Josh smiled, even as he realized how ridiculous he sounded. He was flying first class across the Atlantic, not writing letters with a fountain pen on the Queen Mary.

But if she thought it odd, she didn't show it and within the minute there was the paper and pen, just as requested.

Hope I wasn't snoring, Josh wrote. He tapped the pen against his teeth, then continued.

This is the most amazing thing anyone's ever done for me. Never travelled first before! So comfy. Loads of space. Don't suppose you'd still like to give me your number?? I lost yours in an unfortunate child-and-coffee disaster. No one was injured though! I'll swap your number for mine. J x

With painstaking care, Josh wrote his number at the bottom of the note, then folded it over and wrote across it, *FAO CAPTAIN GUY*. He summoned the flight attendant again.

She took the note with a smile that suggested this wasn't a surprise and disappeared along the cabin. Josh felt utterly calm, which might be the champagne and the travel sickness pill, but the second chance with Captain Guy didn't hurt either.

When the attendant returned she was still smiling and in her hand she held another folded piece of paper. She stooped to hand it to Josh and asked, "More champagne, sir?"

"Yeah…wouldn't mind." His eye on the piece of paper, he asked, "Did I miss lunch, by the way?"

"We'll be serving in five minutes," she said, glancing at the note for just a second. "I'll fetch that champagne."

"Great!" Josh waited for her to head off to wherever they kept their endless supply of champagne, and opened Guy's note.

I hope the cinnamon bun survived the catastrophe! Your number is safely stowed in my terrifyingly efficient phone, away from coffee and children. Make the most of the bubbly! G xx

Josh sighed with relief. Guy had left his number at the bottom of the note, so Josh took out his own phone — sensibly set to flight mode — and entered Guy's number. He read the note several times over, enjoying the easy loops of Guy's writing and hearing the words of the note in Guy's smooth voice. And not just one kiss now but two.

Then he wrote his reply.

Your number now safe in my phone too. Maybe we can meet up while we're both out in Guadeloupe? Might need to escape the wedding party one evening! And yes, the cinnamon bun survived. It was delicious, and maybe one day I'll be able to get you another. J xx

Lunch was unlike anything Josh had ever tasted on board on aircraft before. Washed down with champagne, the salmon pasta he'd ordered tasted as good as any restaurant's — better than some, in fact. The sauce was creamy and light, the salmon buttery and the bread served with it so fresh it might just have come out of the oven. The only thing that improved the experience was the sight of his fairy godmother approaching, another note in her hand.

"From the flight deck," was all she said as she placed it on the table and continued on her way.

Escaping wedding parties is just one of my many uses! Let's see if we can find cinnamon buns in Guadeloupe…or at least have fun trying. G xxx

Three kisses now!
Josh grinned as he wrote his reply.

Lovely warm ones for breakfast? J xxx

He tried to hide his yawn as he waved to the flight attendant.

"Sorry for distracting the pilot," Josh said as he passed her the note.

"Captain Collingwood isn't easily distracted," she replied, with a rather saucy quirk of her perfectly shaped brows. Josh wasn't sure what to make of that, but it seemed like a compliment of sorts. Three kisses, after all.

Captain Collingwood.

Perfect.

Josh snuggled under his blanket again, *Captain Collingwood* repeating in his mind, curling through the darkness behind his eyelids as if Guy himself were writing his name there.

His handsome pilot with three kisses.

* * * *

Josh awoke once the pain in his ears was too hard to ignore. He tried to get back to sleep, but soon realized that his ears hurt because they couldn't be far from landing. He sucked as hard as he could to make his ears pop.

There was a hubbub aboard, people who had been previously quite happy in their seats getting up and fussing around. Josh yawned and folded up his blanket, then spotted another note.

Nothing better after a midnight swim in the Caribbean. G xxxx

"Ladies and gentlemen, this is your captain speaking. We're about to begin our descent into Pointe-à-Pitre, Guadeloupe, very slightly ahead of schedule. It's five to three and it's a beautiful day. On behalf of British Airways, thank you for flying with us today and if anyone knows where to find cinnamon buns in this part of the world, please make yourself known to a member of the crew. The seatbelt signs are now illuminated and my birthday cake's waiting, so let's get our feet on the ground. Cabin crew, prepare for landing."

Josh put his seatbelt on, but imagined hands other than his on the buckle. The experienced, assured hands of Captain Collingwood.

Outside, the perfect blue sea sparkled in the sun, and below he saw an island of dark green and bright, white sand. And flying them safely down through the air, his very own pilot and his four kisses.

And the landing was smooth, just as he'd known it would be—just as everything was in Guy Collingwood's hands, it seemed. There was no scramble for the exits in first class though, no running for the door, because they didn't have to. They were first. And for today, Josh was one of them.

He gathered his bags and made his way along the wide aisle to the door, where the flight crew had gathered. All were neat and unruffled, even after a nine-hour shift, and none was smiling more brightly than Josh's fairy godmother. She acknowledged him with a little bob of her head as he passed and said politely, "Keep that number safe," before she added, "Good afternoon."

"Thanks for looking after me, Teri." With a wink, he added, "And please pass my compliments on to the pilot for a smooth flight."

"Consider it done!" She grinned.

Josh breezed through immigration. He retrieved his suitcase and was out in the sunshine.

Chapter Three

His hotel was on the little island of St Sebastian. Josh tried not to laugh as he thought of all the classical artworks of the saint, his chest bared and the arrows stuck into him, quite incidental to the young man's figure on display.

He was collected with several other island guests first in a minibus then in a speedboat owned by the hotel. Josh ended up squashed in the stern behind a wall of suitcases. But he didn't care a bit. He hadn't felt this relaxed and happy for a long time.

He trailed his fingers in the water as the motorboat bounced over the waves, spray showering up into the air around them like diamonds.

As soon as he'd arrived in his room — in reality, not a room so much as a tiny house on stilts out on the beach — Josh dug out his phone and switched it on. He'd send Captain Guy a short text. Just to say he was on St Sebastian, and the wedding party weren't around until tomorrow, and *would he like to…if he wasn't too busy…meet up?* He knew Guy could be anywhere in Guadeloupe, but still. He wanted to show willing.

Josh stabbed at the screen, then groaned in defeat.

The bloody thing's dead!

Why hadn't he shelled out to get the battery replaced?

And he could see the charger now, still plugged in next to the kettle.

In England.

With a sigh, Josh threw his lifeless phone onto the bed. Tomorrow he could beg a charger from the happy couple. Tonight, he'd get to know his island paradise.

* * * *

No modern technology meant Josh decided to go for a swim. He dived into the inviting waves from his balcony and pulled himself through the water with powerful strokes. He was like a pirate, escaping from his ship.

Josh didn't want to go too far out, so he swam along the coastline. His hotel of little huts and the beach with its palm-leaf-roofed bars passed away from sight, and soon, once he'd taken the small risk of swimming around a low, rocky headland, he saw what seemed to be a private beach.

Josh trod water, taking in the sight of a rather swish house — or was it a hotel? — that he could just about see between the palm trees. It was like his own room on steroids, the entire open front of the house swathed in long, gauzy drapes behind which lights burned. He could just hear music playing — jazz, but he wouldn't hold that against the residents — and wondered if this was the sort of place where a man like Captain Guy Collingwood would stay.

On his jolly.

For his birthday.

Josh was extremely tempted to swim up to the shore and take a look, pretending to be lost. But if it wasn't Captain Guy, and was instead an infuriated tourist who didn't take kindly to strange swimmers arriving on their beach, it might get a bit dicey.

He swam a little closer to the shore, until his feet touched the bottom. Confident that no one could see, Josh whispered, "Just in case you're here, Captain Guy — or wherever the heck you are —!"

Josh kissed his hand and waved. Then, worrying now that maybe someone *had* seen, he swam back to his hut.

* * * *

Josh put on a pair of loose trousers and a dark blue linen shirt. He looked like he'd ram-raided Michael Palin's wardrobe, but the man had style and knew how to dress for tropics. Although Josh wasn't sure he'd wear a panama hat too.

So he wandered off to get some dinner. He didn't much fancy eating alone, but everyone seemed very friendly, and as he wandered barefoot across the beach, his sandals swinging from his hand, he saw one beach bar in particular that looked *very* friendly indeed.

Music carried on the breeze over the sound of cheery conversation and what he could only describe as raucous laughter, but that wasn't the sort of thing to put Josh off. Besides, what was a bit of rowdy fun compared to the tantalizing aroma of food that Josh could smell? His senses were assailed by a heady mix of spices and exotic scents, which combined to draw him closer to the lights of the beach bar. Everything seemed heightened here beneath the Caribbean moon and this evening he wasn't part of the wedding party from England—he was just Josh, out adventuring on his own as he so rarely did at home.

A smiling waiter passed him carrying a steaming platter of seafood, headed for one of the tables that were scattered across the sand, and Josh watched hungrily.

This is the place, he decided. He'd have a private toast to Captain Collingwood's birthday.

As the waiter returned he gave Josh a friendly nod and paused to tell him, "Best bar on the island and the best cook in the Caribbean. If you don't agree by the time we've fed you, it's on the house! Come on, give us a try?"

"Yeah, all right, then!" Josh said. "That seafood looks amazing. Is that the house special?"

"It is tonight." He laid his hand on Josh's shoulder. "Grab a table on the beach, or up at the bar if you're in the party mood. What're you drinking, my friend?"

The sounds of partying and music in the bar were far too tempting to Josh, after spending most of his day alone. "I'm *definitely* in a party mood! What's the local drink?"

"Let me set you up with a glass of ti' punch to get you started." The man slapped his hand to Josh's arm and they began to walk back toward the bar. "Let's get you to a table and put a drink in your hand!"

Josh laughed. "I'm on holiday—bring it on!"

The bar was loud and busy, buzzing with life and energy. Josh absorbed the atmosphere in moments, and said, "Hi there! All right?" to everyone he bumped into. The place seemed to be a mixture of locals and holidaymakers, everyone out enjoying themselves. And Josh decided that he would too.

The platter of food that landed in front of Josh was a banquet of fresh fish and vegetables, rich with aromatic spices. The party was spilling out onto the veranda now and Josh smiled as he heard raucous singing, some 80s hit or another. It was a world away from the forthcoming wedding of the century at which he was best man.

He took a mouthful of coconut rice and realized he'd never tasted anything quite like it before. And certainly not in a place like this. The only way it could've been better was if Guy had been there too.

If only I'd remembered my bloody phone charger…

As the thought entered his head, a woman broke away from the party. She held a bottle of beer in the air, her floaty red dress swishing around her as she pirouetted with the music. She stumbled against Josh's table and, with a hoot of merriment, turned to say in a broad Yorkshire accent, "Sorry, mate!"

At least now Josh didn't have a precious napkin that would be ruined by a jolt against his table.

He looked up and said, "It's okay!" Then he realized he knew her. "You look different — Teri, isn't it? Off the plane!"

"Oh my God!" The flight attendant was no longer immaculate, but quite the opposite. Her face was free of makeup, her hair hanging in unkempt curls about her shoulders. "Floppy fringe Josh!"

Teri blushed immediately, as though she'd said something she shouldn't. "You didn't message back! Guy didn't invite you so you could sit on your lonesome!"

Josh tried and failed to sweep his fringe back from his face. "Did he text me? My phone's been off — the thing's dead and I can't charge it. Is he here? Guy? Is this his party?"

"Don't worry about the fringe." Teri laughed. "It's just — Guy asked me to look out for you to upgrade you." She did a rather passable impersonation of the pilot. "His name's Josh, you can't miss him. He's got a fringe like a poet." Her bottle met his glass with a *chink*. "This is Captain Collingwood's *do* and you're invited!"

Fringe like a poet.

Josh had never written a poem in his life, but he wasn't about to argue with Guy's description of him.

"This place is great!" Josh grinned. "Erm…where's Guy? I know he'll be busy, what with it being his birthday, and there must be loads of his friends here, but I just want to thank him for upgrading me."

And I can't wait to see his smile again.

"He's busy reveling in the attention." Teri replied. "But this'll make his night. I'll give him a shout?"

Her bottle clinked against Josh's glass again and she danced away, into the crowd on the veranda.

Josh dabbed at his cheek, hoping he hadn't managed to get food around his face. His heart pounded as he remembered the pilot he'd met that morning, and who had seen him safely across the Atlantic.

The pilot who had left him a message.

He tried to look casual and not peer keenly after Teri, but it was too tempting not to. Guy was somewhere in the center of the scrum, somewhere in the middle of the 80s tunes.

Josh saw the crowd part a moment before Guy emerged.

Was it possible that he was even more handsome than before?

As much as the pilot's uniform had suited him, seeing Guy relaxed in a loose shirt and cargo shorts, his hair tousled, Josh could only smile at him with a huge, idiotic grin. And Guy wanted to go to dinner with him? He'd even invited him to his birthday party… *How is this possible?* But it was. And, not knowing what else to do, Josh waved to him.

And Guy waved back, his grin as huge but, Josh was sure, far less idiotic than Josh's own.

"Get a new bloody phone." Guy laughed as he reached Josh's table. "You're the hardest man in the islands to track down!"

"Fate has a funny way of forcing us together, doesn't it?" Josh got up from his seat. He wasn't sure if he was supposed to shake hands with Guy, but that seemed rather formal so he leaned forward and gave him a friendly kiss on the cheek. "And at the same time, fate's trying to keep us apart! So great to see you again, Guy. It's brilliant!"

"You're going to join us?" Guy kissed Josh's cheek in return. "But until you've eaten this feast of yours, I'm going to invite myself to your spare seat."

"You're more than welcome to, but are you sure? What about all your mates?"

"Oh, they'll manage without me." Guy settled onto the chair and helped himself to one of the king prawns from Josh's banquet. "So, how do you like St Seb?"

"It's the most beautiful place I've ever seen." Josh scooped some rice onto his spoon and brought it to his mouth. "I went for a swim in the sea earlier, and the water's as warm as a bath! And this place is fantastic — I wish my local was as buzzing as this."

"This is like a little secret island," Guy told him. "Off the beaten track and all the better for it. It's one of those places that you'll never forget, and always come back to. It's a state of mind."

"It's magical," Josh decided. "That must be how we've met again!"

"I like that." Guy nodded, his gaze never leaving Josh's. "The island where magic happens?"

"Definitely." Josh's fringe had fallen forward again, the humidity rendering his hair uncontrollable. But he left it there and peered back at Guy through his fall of hair. As the music went on playing in the bar, Josh asked, "Are you going to take me dancing?"

"On the sand, under the stars." Guy smiled. He reached across the table and touched Josh's hand, letting it linger. "I'll take you dancing."

Josh covered Guy's hand with his own. He had felt something at Guy's touch. A spark, or a tremble, he wasn't sure. "See, I told you this place is magical."

"You're not going to believe me, but I don't make a habit of this."

The noise of the party seemed to have faded, leaving the two of them alone. It was as if their table existed in its own little bubble, where nobody could touch them.

"Nor do I." Josh grinned. He stroked the back of Guy's hand with his fingertip, and he made a point of looking now at the hand that controlled huge airplanes, but at the same time was so graceful. So light.

"Then we're a good match."

Josh wondered if that was true. What would the glamorous, dashing pilot think when he realized that Josh wasn't a poet, but an HR manager from Basingstoke? Although on the magical island of St Sebastian, maybe that wouldn't matter. For as long as they were here, Josh could be whoever he wanted to be—even the sort of man worthy of the handsome Captain Collingwood.

"Shall we have another drink?" Guy gestured toward the bar, which seemed to be all it took to produce two more glasses of punch. "I hope you like birthday cake, because we have a ton of it get through."

"I love birthday cake! Oh, and thanks for the drink." Josh raised his drink. "Cheers! And happy birthday."

"Are you really going to eat *all* of this?" Guy nodded toward the plate. "Can I steal another prawn?"

"Grab a fork, help yourself!" Josh said. "Dig in, mate."

Mate? Hardly the word of a poet.

"So, tell me about Josh?" Guy took a napkin-wrapped bundle from the jar of cutlery on the table. "What do you do when you're not at weddings or generously letting pilots steal your supper?"

"Are you sure you want to know?" Josh swept his troublesome fringe aside and it managed to stay out of the way for all of a couple of seconds before falling over his eye again. "I could tell you I'm a pearl diver who lives in a shack by the sea. It's more interesting than the reality!"

"You could tell me anything you like," Guy agreed. "It won't make you any less gorgeous."

Josh chuckled. He took a sip of his drink for courage, then made his admission. "I live in Basingstoke, near my parents' house, in a nice little flat of my own. My parents are both teachers—Dad's a primary school headmaster, Mum teaches maths in a secondary school. They love caravanning. And I'm an HR manager with an MBA, who'd never been to the Caribbean before. See—a pearl diver would be *far* more interesting!"

"Basingstoke?" Guy blinked, and whatever he was about to say, he seemed to think better of it. He dug his fork into the rice. "In case you were wondering— because I know we pilots have a bit of a rep—I'm single. You might not be wondering, but just in case."

"It's okay. I can imagine there's pilots who make the most of being thousands of miles away from home on a regular basis!" Josh took another mouthful of his drink, then remarked, "And there's probably some HR managers who do too, but I'm not one of them. Single.

I've had boyfriends on and off, but…nothing that's lasted."

"The fools," Guy teased. "This is a very, *very* small island, but if you want someone to show you around…"

"I'd love that! So you're staying on the island then? I'm in one of those huts over there." Josh pointed out into the darkness. "I love it — I dived off the balcony earlier. Never done that before!"

"Me too — the hut, not the diving. I'm just round the headland."

The palace on stilts.

"That place is huge! Have you brought all your mates along plus half the passengers on the plane?" Josh chuckled. "I swam round the headland — wanted to see what was on the other side."

"Just me and a few mates," Guy replied with a smile. "Some of them probably served you your lunch on the plane! Next time you swim past, come up for a drink?"

"Certainly will!" Josh wondered what on Earth that would look like, as he rose from the sea like a masculine Ursula Andress. Looking down at the empty plate, Josh grinned. "That was delicious!"

"Una's *the* best cook you'll ever meet. If she's not catering this wedding of yours, it's a bloody crime." As Guy spoke, the waiter approached their table. "Noah, regards to Madame Mere — she's done it again!"

Noah squeezed Guy's shoulder. "And that's why you *always* come back!" He glanced at Josh and what appeared to be a look of realization crossed his face. Followed quickly by a smile. "And you'll come back too, right?"

Guy looked to Josh, one eyebrow raised.

Josh tried to forget about the enormous figure on his credit card to afford his brief sojourn in paradise. "I'd love to! One day, maybe."

"Captain Guy can stow you away on his plane," Noah told him with a wink.

Guy laughed and slapped Noah's back matily. "I'm sure I can work my BA magic somehow!"

Noah grinned. For a moment, he seemed to forget that he was running the place, then he glanced at the queue at the bar. "Customers are waiting — I'll see you two around." And he headed back behind the bar.

"I guarantee you that Teri won't find her way back to the cabana tonight," Guy confided. "So, do you want to join the party or would you rather have a stroll on the beach? Your choice, it's your first time on St Seb!"

"I wouldn't want to take you away from your party. Not on your birthday. But…" Josh took Guy's hand again. "It's a lovely evening for a stroll."

"My birthday goes on for at least a week. There's plenty of time for celebrations." Guy's fingers twined with Josh's and when he spoke again, his voice was low. "Let's go."

Josh was fairly sure his heart hadn't just skipped a beat but leaped one, and he couldn't quite find the breath to speak. *This is happening. Really.* He closed his eyes for a moment, then opened them again. Guy was still there, still holding his hand.

"Let's go," Josh echoed, and rose from his seat. Together they made their way through the bar and out onto the beach, where the music and laughter seemed louder than ever. The sky was black now and studded with stars, but the air was as warm as the sand beneath their feet and Josh could hear the waves lapping softly at the edge of the shoreline as though in a dream.

He glanced at Guy, his profile picked out in the glow from the strings of lights that draped the bars along the shore. As if confiding a secret, Josh whispered, "I'm glad today has been extra long. Because it's been a brilliant day, hasn't it?"

"It's been perfect." Guy smiled. "I'm just glad you fancied a cinnamon bun this morning."

Josh held Guy's hand a little tighter. "I fancied something else this morning too…"

"Was it a latte, by any chance?" he asked innocently.

"Yes…and this bloke — or should I say, this *guy* who looked *fit as* in his uniform." Josh grinned. "Haven't stopped thinking about him all day."

"I hope I pass muster in my civvies," Guy said casually. He lifted their joined hands and lightly kissed Josh's fingers. "I met this gorgeous chap with a wonderfully floppy fringe. I'm sure he was flirting with me!"

"Do you think so? Whatever gave you that idea?" Josh asked. "And by the way, I think you're even more handsome out of your uniform. I mean…out of your uniform and into your civvies. Although, who am I to say, maybe you're at your most handsome wearing nothing at all!"

"I'm a modest sort of fellow, so I couldn't say," Guy told him, more innocent than ever. "I'd have to give you the casting vote."

"That's very kind of you!" Josh kissed Guy's cheek. He lingered just a moment longer than he had in the bar, breathing in the inimitable scent of him. "You even *smell* gorgeous."

"When I saw you getting on my plane…" Guy turned just a little, so they were facing each other. His free hand came to rest on Josh's hip, gentle and light. "You know I'm just a bit older than you? Quite a bit, really... Is that okay?"

"You told me, you're forty-nine." Josh brushed the edge of Guy's jaw with the back of his hand. "It's fine. Really. It doesn't matter one bit. You're so attractive—I don't care that you're older than me. Do you mind me being younger?"

"Not a bit," he said softly. Then he closed the narrow space between them and put his lips to Josh's, kissing him.

Josh sighed, closing his eyes and enjoying every moment of their kiss. It was gentle, but Josh could feel something else—the promise of heat. He slipped his arms around Guy, holding him close as he allowed the kiss to deepen.

And he hadn't been lying—he really *didn't* do this sort of thing. Then again, he didn't meet men like Guy Collingwood often either, or stroll on moonlit tropical beaches beneath gently waving palm trees. Or at least, he didn't until tonight.

Josh wanted him. Desired him. Needed him. Hadn't even realized until he'd met Guy that he could crave another human being like this. It couldn't just be the beautiful beach—he'd have felt the same if he'd been kissing Guy at the caravan park in Weston Super Mare.

"I need you," Josh whispered, convinced those three words would send Guy running off to his luxury hut.

It sounds too much.

"My place?" Guy's lips moved lower, ghosting over his throat. "Or yours?"

"Mine? It's nearer..." Josh winced. "Sorry...I don't want to sound desperate! It's just...I don't want to waste a second with you."

Because we'll go back to England and I'll be sat in an office while you're flying the globe.

"Lead me to it," Guy decided. "And don't apologize—I feel exactly the same way about you."

"Seriously?" Josh stroked through Guy's luxuriantly thick hair. "Right, come this way...it's the hut with the spotty towel hanging over the balcony!"

"Of course it is." Guy laughed. "I should've guessed!"

"Just through here..." Josh led Guy by the hand, unlocking a gate that took them onto the hotel's part of the beach. His room was close by, and Josh headed up the steps to the door, fumbling as he tried to put the key in the lock. The soft touch of Guy's lips on the back of his neck didn't help him focus either, nice though it was, and he was happy to feel Guy's hand close over his, guiding the key into the lock.

The metal finally bit and Josh turned the key. For a moment, he panicked, convinced he'd left his room in a mess, but the thought vanished. Because he was going to take the captain to his bed, and nothing else mattered at that moment.

By the time the door closed behind them, they were in each other's arms once more, everything else forgotten. This was the best room in the world, Josh decided. It had to be.

He tugged at Guy's shirt, trying to pull it over his head, and tried to take his own off at the same time, and kicked off his sandals and got into a muddle. "Sorry..." he whispered with a chuckle against Guy's neck. "I'm...not normally this clumsy!"

"Blame the jet lag," Guy told him smoothly. He kissed Josh again, nimbly unfastening the buttons on the dark blue shirt Josh had chosen earlier, when he had expected a quiet night with his own company. Without breaking the kiss, Guy slid his hands over Josh's chest, caressing and exploring.

Josh breathed carefully now, trying not to get too carried away. He slowly unbuttoned Guy's shirt and caressed his firm chest as it appeared from beneath the soft fabric. Josh had never gone to bed with a man of forty-nine before, and he hadn't known what to expect, but Guy's figure was pretty impressive.

And as confident as Guy was, Josh suspected that he probably knew it too.

"Pearl diving suits you," Guy decided against Josh's lips. "You're bloody perfect."

"And flying planes certainly suits *you*." Josh caressed between their bodies, down Guy's stomach to the top of his shorts. "Do you want me to...?"

"I would love you to." He grinned, shrugging off his shirt to reveal strong arms. *Arms made for embracing HR managers.* "Would you be more comfortable on the bed?"

"Yes." Josh's room wasn't particularly large and he reached the mosquito net from where they stood and parted it. "I pretend they're the diaphanous curtains of a luxurious four-poster bed."

"What do you mean, *pretend*?" Guy winked. "A man could get happily lost in a bed like this, especially if he had a good-looking chap from Basingstoke with him!"

Josh laughed as he led Guy through the curtains. "Welcome to my glamorous bed!"

"A perfect bed!" Guy bounced down onto the mattress and drew Josh with him. This time the embrace that followed was even closer, their torsos pressed together. Josh felt those elegant fingers in his hair, Guy's skin warm against his.

Josh was vaguely aware of the sound of the fan turning in the warm air, and of the gentle swish of the waves against the beach. But above that he heard their kisses, and the rustle of their clothes as they caressed.

He unbuttoned Guy's shorts and reached inside. A soft gasp of approval escaped Guy's lips and he dropped his mouth to Josh's throat, pressing heated kisses to his neck. Those arms were around him now, holding him in a tender embrace. *My captain's arms.*

With his other hand, Josh inched down Guy's shorts. He glanced at him and whispered, "See...you're so handsome without your clothes!"

"I'm very pleased to hear it," Guy replied, apparently as confident naked as he was in uniform. *And why not?* "And entirely at your disposal, of course!"

Josh slipped his arms free of his shirt and dropped it onto the bed, then kissed Guy more intensely as he stroked Guy's erection. He roamed his other hand across Guy's toned stomach and chest, and firm thighs. This was turning out to be quite an evening.

And it was only getting better, he realized, as Guy's fingers undid his belt and trousers. For a moment his hands rested on Josh's waist, then he slid them beneath the waistband of both his trousers and boxers, cupping the curve of Josh's buttocks.

Josh moaned. "I want you. I want to know what it's like to be in experienced hands."

"I'm sure we can teach each other a few things," Guy whispered, nibbling softly at Josh's earlobe as he teased one fingertip down the cleft of his buttocks. "And if there's anything your captain can do for you..." His mouth moved lower, trailing kisses over Josh's chest until the tip of his tongue flicked over one nipple.

Josh arched his back against Guy's mouth, moaning as a tremble of pleasure rippled through him. He wove his fingers through Guy's hair to hold him close against him. "I want my captain to enjoy his birthday."

There was a certain casual artistry in the manner in which Guy drew the tip of his tongue from Josh's nipple down to his navel and at the same time stripped his trousers and boxers from him. It was like a magician performing a very saucy trick. Only then did he kiss his way back up to Josh's mouth, and together they lay beneath the softly turning fan as they embraced, their legs entwined and their lips lost in kisses.

Their kisses were heated and passionate, but underneath, Josh sensed an alluring tenderness. They'd only just met, and there was no way that Guy would spare him a thought once Josh had gone back to being a very ordinary office worker, but Josh didn't care.

Not tonight. Tonight he was Guy's poet and pearl diver. Tonight he was in paradise.

And Guy's kisses were as leisurely and confident as everything else about him seemed to be. One elegant hand rested on Josh's bottom again, the other softly tangled in his hair, and with every touch, it seemed as though they had all the time in the world. If this was an experienced man, Josh certainly approved.

Josh broke from their kiss. Still stroking Guy's erection, he whispered, "How would you like your pearl-diver poet?"

"Right here." With one movement Guy turned onto his back, pulling Josh on top of him. He winked and said with a touch of mischief, "I want to see you enjoying the ride."

Unexpected. But Josh wasn't about to complain. Guy looked ridiculously louche and attractive, his tousled hair so dark against the pillow.

"And I've got a fantastic view from up here, Captain." Josh swept back his fringe, then winked toward the bedside table. "I'm a careful traveler. Everything we need is in there…when the moment comes."

"The *moment*?" Guy's words were more mischievous than ever, and he reached one hand out to playfully tease Josh's nipple. "I hope I'm not quite as old as *that*!"

"You're gorgeous," Josh murmured. "And maybe we'll have several moments!"

"I'm sure of it." As Guy spoke, he finally took Josh's erection in his hand and began to caress him. There was that confidence again, the firm, gentle strokes not faltering when he drew Josh down for more kisses, just a little more urgently than before.

Josh sighed into their kiss, his hips moving of their own volition against Guy's thrusts. Guy was so assured in everything, just as Josh had hoped. He felt Guy's free hand come to rest on his buttock and heard that glorious voice murmur, "Let me know when you feel like *the moment* has come, darling."

"I wanted you the moment I saw you," Josh said, "the moment I heard your voice."

He propped himself up, his hand beside Guy's face, and gazed down at him. In the soft light, Guy was the most desirable man on the planet at that moment, and a tremble of heat ran through Josh's body that Guy couldn't have mistaken.

"So what," Guy asked softly, "did my *careful traveler* pack?"

Only slightly disentangling their bodies, Josh reached across to the bedside table and took out a box of condoms and a tube. He laid them on the bed, blushing even though he knew there was nothing to be embarrassed about. But there was something so frank about those items. So practical.

Josh grinned. "I like to be prepared. That's the thing with travel — you never know who you might meet."

"Very true," was Guy's sage reply. "They let all sorts of rogues fly triple sevens these days."

Rogue. Josh grinned even more. He pushed himself up to sit across Guy's legs and gazed at him appreciatively as he lay there. "I can't resist a terrible pun," Josh admitted. "Can I prepare you for take-off?"

"I love a bad pun," Guy assured him with a nod. "It must be a pilot thing."

Josh prepared Guy with deftness. He linked his fingers with Guy's and brought them to his lips to kiss them. "Ready for take-off, Captain Guy."

"I won't welcome you aboard." He grinned, running one fingertip over Josh's lips. "Unless you really want me to."

With another of those louche winks Guy closed his hand over Josh's hip and lifted him just a little, the tip of his erection teasing against Josh's body. An unexpected and rather loud groan escaped Josh's lips at that moment, and he tried not to giggle. This was perfect, so perfect that as their bodies joined, Josh allowed himself to daydream that this wasn't just a holiday fling.

Guy responded with a fairly spirited groan too, but unlike Josh, he couldn't hold back the slight hint of laughter that followed it. "Sorry." He beamed, his blue eyes shining in the dim light. "But you're *wonderful.*"

Josh opened his mouth to reply, but he couldn't speak—pleasure robbed him of words and he moaned at the sensation as he moved against Guy. He held Guy at the waist, feeling the strength in his lover and wishing, greedily, that they could have more than just this one night.

Guy's hand returned to Josh's erection, his rhythm matching the pace of his hips. He gazed up at Josh, the expression on his handsome face nothing short of smoldering. Captain Collingwood—*his* Captain Collingwood, for tonight at least—was the most marvelous thing he'd ever seen, his eyes glittering, his full lips slightly parted and a faint sheen of perspiration on the toned planes of his body.

And he definitely knew what he was doing. Every move was confident, accomplished, drawing out their intense pleasure. It was no mad dash to the finishing line but a smooth ride.

Josh tossed his head to sweep his hair from his eyes and gave voice to the moans that were building in his throat, not caring if anyone overheard.

Guy's fingertips found Josh's nipple again, gently rolling the stiff peak between finger and thumb. Each thrust was a little harder too, in answer to Josh's moans of pleasure.

"Flip me over," Josh sighed. "I want to feel you from behind."

And Guy even managed to make the unexpected change in their position seem like choreography, withdrawing for just as long as it took to settle Josh on the cool sheets. As their bodies joined again, Josh could feel Guy's chest against his back and the heat of his breath a moment before his lips pressed a hungry kiss to Josh's neck. He really was in Guy's arms now, safe in the warmth of his embrace.

They were more deeply joined than ever, their coupling carnal yet tender. Elegant, even. Josh felt so free, so unfettered, but he didn't know and couldn't work out whether it was his lover or the warm tropical night that made him feel that way.

Then Guy whispered his name and somehow, it seemed like the most decadent sound in the world. Or at least, it did until he took a gentle nip of Josh's earlobe and breathed, "Darling…"

That gorgeous voice vibrated through Josh—he felt its timbre in every limb. Josh turned his head, seeking out Guy's lips with his own. "Captain..."

The kiss they shared seemed to go on and on, filled with the same breathless need that surged through Josh's veins. And Guy must have sensed it too, he was sure, because he could feel it in every powerful thrust of his hips and jerk of his wrist.

Josh trembled as his orgasm began to rush through him.

"Captain Collingwood!" he moaned. "You gorgeous rogue!"

"*Your* gorgeous rogue," Guy corrected, his voice low and breathless. "You feel wonderful like this..."

Do I?

Josh tried to reply but could only manage another moan as his orgasm finally broke. Only then did Guy let himself go, his glorious voice caught in a gasp of exertion as pleasure claimed him. Josh drank in the tensing of Guy's muscles against him, and allowed himself to drop against the bed. He reached behind him to caress Guy's side.

"That was...bloody hell..." Josh turned his head again, smiling. Guy's answering smile was nothing short of dreamy and he took Josh's hand as he kissed him.

"This is turning out to be one hell of a birthday," he said. "Thanks to this pearl-diving poet I know."

Josh chuckled. "While I'm here, I'm a pearl-diving poet! Happy birthday, Captain."

"It's the best one I can remember." Guy beamed and added playfully, "You gorgeous thing."

"Can we hug?" Josh asked. "Just for a little while."

"You read my mind." Guy turned Josh in his arms and drew him close.

Josh murmured happily as he wrapped his arms around Guy. They were a hot, sweaty mess, and it was fantastic. "Do you want to stay the night? You can, if you want to. The bed's big enough."

"I'd love to," he sighed, snuggling Josh against his chest. "And if you have time—if you want to—I'd still like to take you to dinner one night. Wedding duties permitting, of course."

"I'm sure I can sneak off!" Josh tangled a strand of Guy's hair around his finger. The few silver hairs caught the light. "It might be a bit boring for you, seeing as you won't know anyone, but…if I can convince my mate to let you squeeze onto the top table as my plus one at the reception, would you like to?"

Of course you won't, but I wish you would.

But Guy smiled and told him, "I'd love to! Just let me know when and where. And the dress code, so I know whether I need to iron a good shirt."

"It's penguin outfits as far as the eye can see, I'm afraid." Josh grinned. "You could rock up in your uniform—although I don't suppose you'd want to get sand in it. And…I bet you'd look cute in a bow tie."

"I'll have to call in some favors." Guy quirked his eyebrow, the gesture filled with mischief. "I don't generally travel with my dicky."

Whether Guy turned up in a tux or his uniform, he'd look stunning, Josh was certain. "Surprise me, *darling*."

"I might even swim back in the morning." Guy nodded. "Pretend to be James Bond!"

"You should!" Josh kissed Guy's cheek. In the quiet, he heard the waves sweeping against the beach and washing around the stilts under his room. "Hey, I don't suppose you'd like to go for a dip now?"

"Shall we? Can I dive off the balcony too?"

Josh loved Guy's sense of adventure and fun. "Absolutely! And no swimming shorts required, either."

"I love it, let's go!"

Josh parted the mosquito net and climbed out of the bed. He held his hand out to Guy. Guy reached up and wrapped his fingers around Josh's.

"Lead me to it."

They crossed the room, stepping over their discarded clothes. Josh drew back the locks and they were out on the balcony. His spotty towel, which had drawn them to the room like a beacon, flapped in the sea breeze over the balcony rail. Josh slipped his arm around Guy's waist and stared out across the gentle waves that were studded with the reflection of the stars.

"It's a fab view during the day, but *this* is magical," Josh decided. "I suppose you sometimes see this from up there? You must see some really beautiful things." He pointed upward, imagining Captain Collingwood at the controls of a plane.

"The world looks very different from all the way up there," Guy told him, wrapping his arm around Josh's waist in turn. "We all have our favorite routes, but this one's definitely mine. Looking down on the islands, it feels like coming home. This is the best place in the world."

"I'm definitely warming to it!" Josh said. "Okay, if we both stand on the top step we can dive in at the same time."

Guy's answer was an utter smooch of a kiss, the sort of cinematic snog guaranteed to make the recipient's heart skip at least one beat. Then he squeezed Josh's hand and grinned, "Come on, there's nothing like skinny-dipping in the Caribbean!"

They went to the top step and Josh grinned at Guy before staring out at the waves again. "On the count of three?"

"Count us in, then *chocks away*, as we used to say in the RAF!" Guy lifted Josh's hand and kissed it.

RAF. Josh's mind conjured up a historically inaccurate yet no less pleasing image of Guy in a Second World War flight jacket, a jaunty silk scarf around his neck. Guy's chiseled good looks were perfect for the part. But Josh decided not to let on about that particular thought, and instead counted them in.

"One...two..." Josh wobbled forward slightly on the step and chuckled as he regained his balance. "Two and a half...three!"

The dive was rather less accomplished than either might have hoped because, at the last, the two men didn't let go of each other's hands. Instead they hit the wonderfully warm water at the same moment and, as they surfaced, Guy pulled Josh into his arms and kissed him.

Josh entwined his fingers in Guy's hair as their kiss went on. The warm water lapping against their bodies made the moment even more sensual than Josh had expected it could be.

This was like the most wonderful dream he could hope to imagine, but Captain Guy was very real indeed. Josh stroked his hands down from Guy's head, down his back, finally resting them against his buttocks.

"Not a bad way to spend an evening!" Josh grinned.

"Just so you know, my bedroom's the one on the veranda," Guy informed him. So it *had* been Guy listening to jazz earlier, and Josh had blown a kiss in precisely the right direction. "In case you ever fancy dropping in?"

"If you don't mind a dripping wet pearl-diver poet with a floppy fringe paying you a visit."

"I don't think I can imagine anything better than that." Guy's arms tightened just a little around Josh's waist. "Any time you like, darling."

"How can I refuse?" Josh kissed him. Under the water, he circled his toes against Guy's ankle and his elegant foot.

"So we could swim…or we could" — Guy punctuated the sentence with another of those smoochy kisses — "just do this. I don't want to let you go."

Josh still couldn't quite believe that any of this was happening. Guy was still there — he wasn't a mirage. Josh caressed the small of Guy's back, circling his fingertips against his skin, as if convincing himself that Guy was real. A man as gorgeous as Guy, who wanted to have Josh in his arms.

"We can swim another day," Josh said. "Today, we can do this. Because *this* is very nice indeed."

And it was, because what could be better than this? An experienced man, just as Josh had wanted, with silver in his hair and laughter in his eyes and heat in his kisses. And far sexier than James Bond ever was.

They went on kissing, the sea washing around them with its own warm caresses.

"We're going to need a shower before we get back into bed," Josh said. "It's not the biggest shower cubicle I've ever seen in my life, but I'm sure we can squeeze in."

"Just for future reference in case you ever fancy it, I have a rather roomy spa bath at my disposal," Guy purred. "But I'd love to squeeze into a steamy shower with you."

"I am *definitely* going round yours. It sounds amazing!" Josh gripped Guy's buttocks tightly. "By the way, you have *such* a great arse. I have to tell you that, even though I'm sure you know."

And of course Guy's response to that was to tense the muscles in that gorgeous bottom beneath Josh's hand.

"I'm very modest, you know. We pilots always are."

"Absolutely!" Josh said. "Shall we head to the shower?"

"If you were casually wondering, I do still have the RAF gear," Guy teased, kissing him softly. "It's at home in Farnham, but that's not too much of a trek from Basingstoke."

"How have we not met before?" Josh shook his head. The thought of Guy in RAF uniform, even if it didn't involve a cheeky silk scarf, was a very welcome image indeed. "Well, apart from the fact that most of the time you're thousands of feet up in the air."

"But not *all* the time." He felt Guy's hands slide down his back, tender and assured. They came to rest on his bottom. "And even HR managers must get the odd day off?"

"Yes, sometimes I'm allowed to escape the never-ending treadmill of performance management and resilience training." Josh poked out his tongue. "Thrilling as that all is," he deadpanned.

"I'm trying, in my uncharacteristically clumsy way, to ask if you'd like to do something when we're back in England," Guy admitted. "And feel free to say no — we can still enjoy St Seb's!"

Josh grinned. If their holiday fling could continue at home, he wouldn't mind at all. "Are you sure? Like a date? Because if you *are* sure, I'd love to!"

"Fantastic!" Guy kissed his nose. "It'll be a bit less sunny, but no less fun!"

"I have a very tiny shower at home too," Josh told him. "And a rubber duck on the bathroom windowsill. I'll have to introduce you."

"I can't wait." He beamed.

The sea breeze was growing more intense, the waves building. Josh grabbed his towel before it blew off the balcony railing. "Think we'd better go indoors now!"

Together they climbed from the water and onto the beach, Guy still holding Josh's hand. This felt so absurdly natural, as if they had known each other for years. They went back into the hut, and once in the compact bathroom, Josh drew Guy into the shower and let the cool water splash over them. He was in Guy's arms again, held safe and close to that strong chest.

Guy pressed his lips to Josh's and kissed him, long and deep and filled with promise.

Would they see each other again in England? As Josh explored the softness of Guy's mouth, and felt the tenderness in his kiss, he hoped so. More than anything, he hoped so.

"Tomorrow," Guy murmured against his lips, "I'm buying you a charger for that bloody phone of yours."

"That'll come in handy." Josh brushed his hand over Guy's body, trying to remember each freckle, each curve. "Would you like some soap?"

"Would you like to apply it?" he teased. "Because if you would, the answer's yes."

Josh popped open the shower gel and spread it onto his hands. Wonderful botanical scents rose up into the steamy air. Then he smoothed his palms over Guy's chest. He was fairly sure that he detected Guy tensing his muscles under his touch, and Josh grinned at the thought of such a handsome man peacocking just for him.

"Is that nice?" Josh asked. "I got this at the airport too! It's a bit posh, isn't it?"

"Well, a chap should treat himself when he's flying to Guadeloupe." Guy's skin was slippery and warm when they embraced, fragrant and fizzing with bubbles. "Cinnamon buns are just the start of it!"

Josh chuckled. He couldn't remember a time he'd had more fun with someone he'd known for barely a day. "Buns! You have *very* nice buns. Sorry…I'm being rude."

"You're very rude," Guy agreed, beaming. He took the shower gel and squeezed it decadently onto Josh's chest, running his hands through the bubbles. "And the best buns on this island!"

"Nice and firm. Just for you," Josh purred. He closed his eyes, enjoying the sensation of Guy's caresses and the water raining down on them. And now it wasn't only Josh's buttocks that were *nice and firm*.

"Would you like me to give you the benefit of my *experience*?" Guy teased, stroking his hands lower. "Nice and firm suits you."

Josh shivered with anticipation. "Go on, then…"

With one more kiss, Guy dropped to his knees before Josh. He blinked up at him through the water. "You're glorious, you know."

Josh smiled down at him. He'd never been described as *glorious* before, and certainly not in a voice that sounded like velvet. The word rebounded inside Josh's head as he gazed down at Guy.

Resting his hands on Guy's shoulders, Josh said, "You make me *feel* glorious."

"You should." Guy stroked Josh's buttocks. He shifted forward just a little then drew the tip of his tongue along Josh's erection, teasing him. "See? *Glorious*."

Josh moaned and ran his hand through Guy's hair. "You're magnificent," he murmured.

This wasn't the sort of thing that happened to Josh, yet here he was, an airline pilot on his knees before him, dotting long, slow kisses to his body and massaging his buttocks with a *very* confident touch. Eventually Guy took Josh's erection between his lips and slowly, tenderly, began to move.

My captain.

Josh watched Guy through half-closed eyes. The man was exquisite and *his*, and maybe not just for their stay. Josh moved his hips gently against Guy, soon finding a rhythm between them that seemed to have always been there.

Guy somehow knew just how to please him, as though they'd known each other for years, not just one day. His hands were so assured in the massage, his mouth so soft, tongue and lips working against Josh's body as the water showered down over them.

Murmuring his lover's name, for the second time that evening Josh climaxed. He leaned back against the shower tiles, smiling like a fool because he couldn't remember feeling this happy before.

"Captain Collingwood, you're the finest pilot who ever flew."

"I'm having the most wonderful night." Guy rocked back on his knees and looked up at him. "With the most wonderful man."

"I'm so glad we've met," Josh said. He grinned — the sparkle in Guy's eyes warmed him. As he watched, Guy rose to his feet, never breaking their gaze.

Glorious.

"Can I take you back to bed, darling?"

Josh held his arms out to Guy. "I'd love that."

Guy gathered Josh into his arms as though he was a groom crossing the threshold. Josh snuggled against Guy's chest, feeling those firm muscles again. Guy reached up and turned off the water then carried him from the bathroom and back to the bed.

Our bed.

Josh pretended it was a luxurious four-poster bed, because in Guy's arms that was exactly what it seemed to be, not a basic double bed draped with mosquito nets. *Everything* seemed brighter, more burnished somehow, with Guy.

Guy paused at the bed to kiss Josh, then laid him down on the sheets. He watched Guy settle beside him, rivulets of water on his broad shoulders.

"Hold me," Josh whispered. Guy enfolded him in his strong arms, cradling him to his chest.

"Thank you," he sighed. "This has been the best birthday I've ever had."

Josh blinked away the droplets of water that still hung in his eyelashes. He wondered if he and Guy would still know each other by the time his next birthday rolled around. "Even if you didn't get the cinnamon bun?"

"I've got you instead, darling." Guy kissed his hair. "What else could I want?"

Josh ran his finger down the side of Guy's cheek. There was such sincerity in Guy, which almost seemed at odds with his unassailable confidence. But Josh supposed that the person he was seeing now was something close to the real Guy Collingwood. A tender, sweet man, packaged within the delicious outer wrapping of an assured and glamorous pilot.

He had never known anyone quite like him.

Still holding Josh, Guy pulled the cool sheet over them. Then he whispered, "I don't want to go to sleep. Is that terribly silly?"

"No, not at all!" Josh rested his cheek against Guy's, feeling his breath warm against his skin. "But we have all of the time here on St Sebastian, and all the time we like once we're home."

"Autumn in England suddenly seems a lot brighter," Guy replied. "Don't you think?"

Josh nodded, grinning. He certainly hadn't been expecting a romance. "Long walks through the fallen leaves — if you like that sort of thing."

Would a glamorous long-haul pilot enjoy something so pedestrian?

"How terribly bored would you be if I suggested Richmond Park?" Guy kissed his hair. "The deer are always worth a wander."

"I'd love that," Josh whispered against Guy's chest, his voice slow with advancing sleep.

"Then we'll do it," he heard his lover murmur, his lips still resting soft against Josh's hair. "Kick some autumn leaves around."

"And go for a cinnamon bun afterward." As Josh closed his eyes, his lashes brushed Guy's chest. "Night-night, Captain Collingwood…"

"Goodnight, darling," his captain whispered. "Sleep tight."

Chapter Four

Josh awoke to the sound of the waves and the distant call of gulls. Somewhere, someone was laughing. He had no idea what time it was, and he opened one eye, for a moment wondering how he'd managed to fit a four-poster bed into his flat.

Then all of the events of yesterday came back to him in one go, and Josh grinned against his pillow.

Wow.

"Good morning." There was that voice, as smooth as silk, close against Josh's ear. "Sleep well?"

Josh turned, his lips just brushing against Guy's face. The fact that Guy had stayed and not done an early flit pleased Josh more than he could say. "Morning...I did sleep well, thanks. Did you?"

"I had some very nice dreams," he admitted, slipping his arm around Josh's waist. "And managed to secure us an especially decadent breakfast, which should be waiting on the balcony whenever we can bring ourselves to get out of bed."

Josh put his arm around Guy in return and gazed at the tousled-haired pilot, taking in the flecks of gold in his sparkling blue eyes.

"You get better and better! Handsome *and* able to magic breakfast out of thin air." Josh sighed. "I don't want to get out of bed. I want to spend the whole of my week here with you."

"Well, let's barricade the doors and keep very quiet. I won't tell" — Guy kissed Josh's nose — "if you don't."

"Not a word, promise." Josh passed his lips over Guy's then kissed him, very softly. But as they were naked and entwined in bed, their kiss began to deepen. He felt Guy's hands stroking his back, a perfect combination of heat and tenderness, the same hands that had safely piloted them halfway across the world just twenty-four hours earlier.

Josh roamed his hands across Guy, sighing into their kiss with appreciation of his body. He sighed even more as he finally slid down to Guy's erection and feathered his fingertips along it. An answering sigh escaped Guy's lips as his hands came to rest on Josh's buttocks, cupping them with obvious relish.

Josh grinned. To think that *this* man wanted him... How could it be true?

He broke from their kiss for long enough to say, "I don't suppose there's time before breakfast to..." Guy was so sophisticated, Josh thought for a moment to choose the right words. "Have another *moment*?"

"Breakfast can wait," Guy said. "Don't you think?"

"I think so, yes." Josh shifted a little, bringing Guy on top of him. "Like this?"

"Perfect," his lover whispered, reaching out for bedside table where Josh's *travel essentials* waited. He was as assured as ever, barely breaking their kisses as he rolled the condom over his erection. In fact, they seemed deeper than they had been, and Josh faintly heard the tube landing back on the table before Guy's hands were on his body again.

Josh stretched one arm up above his head on the pillows. He caressed Guy's side, enjoying the sensation of strength in him.

And he's mine.

For St Sebastian, for the deer park…

There was such tenderness in Guy as he brought their bodies together, despite the power Josh felt in him. He closed his hand around Josh's against the pillow and ducked his head for another kiss, sinking against him as he did.

Josh crossed his legs around Guy, feeling so close to him that it was almost as if they were melting into one. There would be many mornings like this, he hoped.

Josh was no blushing innocent and he had a suspicion that Captain Guy *certainly* wasn't, but here, in the dappled sunlight, was something new. A sense of something so ridiculously right, so absolutely perfect that it seemed almost absurd. And wonderful.

"Guy…" Josh said against Guy's cheek, trying not to graze him with his morning stubble. "You're amazing."

"It's a pilot thing," Guy deadpanned, then added with a playful wink, "That's a joke, don't worry."

Josh chuckled as he tightened his hand with Guy's. He rocked his hips with Guy's movements, the bed beginning to creak as Josh moaned with pleasure.

A pilot thing.

A thing for a pilot, maybe.

Guy's body moved with Josh, their gasps and sighs mingling together, both somehow made of sensation. Every kiss seemed deeper than the last, every embrace tighter and the world outside seemed to melt away, everything that mattered here in this small room.

He was just the sort of man that Josh could fall in love with.

Josh smiled at the thought. If what they had could work in the Hampshire drizzle, then love would follow, Josh was certain.

And surely pilots must fall in love too.

Guy's fingers closed around Josh's erection, his hand matching their rhythm and pace. He caught Josh's earlobe softly between his teeth and whispered, "You *are* glorious, never forget."

Josh chuckled, but the sound transformed into a moan at Guy's touch. "I don't want this to end," Josh murmured.

"It doesn't have to," Guy whispered. "Not if we don't want it to."

"You're such a romantic," Josh replied, ruffling Guy's hair. Was Josh, though? Sometimes, maybe. And with Guy, he couldn't help but be.

"Someone has to be." Guy smiled, touching his nose to Josh's. "We're a dying breed!"

Josh grinned. Guy had made their encounter so sweet. Two men, meeting for the first time, promising each other romance only a day later.

"I'd like to be a romantic too," Josh admitted. "Can I try it out on you?"

"Darling, I would *love* you to!"

"I'll try my best!" Josh tightened his legs around Guy as if giving him a hug. A particularly saucy one at that.

Darling. Guy made it sound like the most decadent word on earth. Romantic wasn't quite Josh, but with Captain Guy, it could be.

Josh kissed him, and pleasure built in him again. His whole body felt alive and his veins seemed to be filled with light, as bright as the sun outside. Josh's hips bucked against Guy's and he moaned his name, again and again, until the words merged into a sigh.

As the moments after that peak of pleasure ebbed away, and they lay together, their limbs entwined, Josh felt completely at peace. Guy's kisses grew more relaxed, though his embrace was as strong as ever, and he whispered, "That's a hell of a wake up."

"Let's do that again sometime." Josh smiled. He half-closed his eyes and listened to the soft sound of Guy's breathing, the throb of the fan as it turned in the warm air above them, and the constant roll of the sea.

"Name the day," Guy said sleepily. "And I'll be there."

Josh drew shapes on Guy's shoulder with his fingertips. "The wedding party are arriving later this afternoon... I'll have to go and see them, can't let Groomzilla down, but maybe later — I could slip away. I could come round yours?"

"You'll find me out on the veranda, sipping *rhum agricole* and looking very smug indeed." Guy smiled. "Whenever you like, darling, just drop round."

"You can count on it." Josh kissed Guy's cheek. Guy had the look of a man who was content to loaf, but Josh was thinking about the breakfast that awaited them. If they were going to spend several hours in bed, Josh wanted to make sure he'd eaten. "Darling? You mentioned breakfast."

"Did I?" He lifted his head, his expression nothing short of dreamy. "Do you have a robe I can borrow? I'm not in the mood for pesky old clothes!"

"Yeah, there's a couple of toweling robes in the bathroom." Josh kissed Guy's forehead. "Let me go and get them and we can be *almost* decent!"

"I shall lounge until you return," Guy decided. "Pilots are always experts in lounging."

"First-class lounge!" Josh quipped. He slipped out of the bed and went into the bathroom, returning with two plush dressing gowns, each with a small embroidered palm tree on the chest pocket. Josh laid one down on the bed for Guy. "Here you are, Captain."

"Oh, they're very *us*!"

Us.

Guy threw back the sheet and finally climbed out of bed. He stretched his arms above his head, then ruffled his already tousled hair. "Do I look a fright?"

Josh bit his lip, trying to rein in his smile. *He's mine.* "You're the sexiest thing I've ever seen."

"You bloody gorgeous liar." Guy laughed. "But I love it anyway!"

"It's a shame to hide that gorg body, but…" Josh tied on his robe and did a twirl. "I look all fluffy!"

No doubt with Josh's words ringing in his ears, Guy tied his a little less securely, leaving just a tantalizing glimpse of his tan chest. Then he took Josh in his arms and said, "You're very cuddly like this!"

"A little bear to hug in bed!" Then Josh realized what he'd said. "I mean, I'm clearly not a bear as in some beardy leatherman—I'm your own personal teddy bear to cuddle up to at night."

"Oh, right." Guy was suddenly grave. "The thing is, when I'm not flying, I prefer to be a leather-clad Grizzly Adams. Is that a problem?"

Chuckling, Josh rubbed Guy's stubble. "I'm sure you could work the look!"

"Well, *naturally*!" He laughed. "The off-duty me is basically this, don't worry!"

"Pottering about Farnham in your elegant toweling robe?" Josh led them out onto the balcony. He stood on the threshold, absorbing the sound of the sea and the heat from the sun. He squeezed Guy's hand and smiled.

"I do a lot of pottering. And I should warn you that I'm a car nut." Guy closed his eyes, breathing deeply. "Just so you know!"

"Bet you drive something more zippy than my Fiat 500. You probably drive the car equivalent of a jumbo jet."

"In 1953, Grandpa Collingwood bought a Jag XK120 in British racing green," Guy told him, a nostalgic look in his eyes. "Twenty years later, he gave it to my pa and twenty years after that, my pa gave it to me." His smile faltered, then returned. "It's a Collingwood family heirloom really!"

"Fantastic! You'll have to take me for a spin." Josh supposed there was a niece or nephew somewhere who would drive the Collingwood Jag once Guy was ready to pass it on. But Josh had a feeling that wouldn't be for a while.

"Oh, believe me, I will." He led Josh out to the table, where covered dishes awaited and, Josh noticed, what looked like a champagne bottle protruding from a silver bucket of ice. "We'll chuck the hood down and hit the open road!"

Josh pictured Guy's hands on the wheel, and could hear the purr of the engine. He sat down at the table and lifted the lid from one of the dishes.

"Cinnamon buns!"

"Courtesy of Una, who also cooked your supper last night!" Guy took the bottle from the ice. "Should I mix up a Buck's Fizz?"

"Go on!" Josh helpfully lined up the glasses, ready. He watched Guy tear the foil and release the cage. Then he took the cork and, as though he did this all the time, popped it from the neck of the bottle.

And it was so decadent, so perfect, that Josh felt that skip in his heart again.

"And if your chums are getting wed on St Seb's, it'll be Una's husband, Pierre, doing the service!" He poured out what Josh knew *had* to be fresh orange juice from a jug on the table, then added champagne. "Cheers!"

"Cheers!" Josh settled in his chair. He squinted out to sea and sighed happily at the sparkling sapphire waves. And Guy was right there beside him, gazing out at the ocean. He reached across and put his hand on Josh's knee, saying nothing.

I don't need to.

Josh covered Guy's hand with his own and entwined their fingers. It was odd to think that thousands of miles away across the ocean, England with its gray skies and drizzle was waiting for them. But back in England, they could be cozy beside a fireplace together and keep each other warm.

"And here's to the happy couple." Guy raised his glass again. "They've got the best best man they could hope for!"

Josh raised his glass too. "To Rey and Stella!"

"Rey and Stella!" Guy repeated. "May they sail happily into the sunset!"

"Or even fly back on your plane!" Josh bit into one of the buns. It was still warm. "Bloody hell, this is better than the one in the airport!"

"Una's magic like that. One day, if I dare, I'd like to wake up to this view every morning." Guy squeezed Josh's knee. "I've defended the realm and ticked off every plane I ever dreamed about—I've earned a bit of sunshine. Wouldn't it be something?"

"To live out here?" Josh gazed dreamily out at the view, then gazed dreamily at Guy. "Can you take early retirement or would you work out here?"

"There used to be a marvelous little island-hopping bird out here, one chap and a couple of planes," Guy recalled. "He just retired and nobody's taken it over so there's a gap in the market..." He laughed. "The problem is, I have zero business nous and no interest in admin. A sure-fire recipe for financial disaster!"

"Oh yeah, you want to be careful!" Josh nodded. "You wouldn't want to invest all your assets and overlook something crucial but not all that obvious, and...you'd be left with nothing but sand in your shoes and a winning smile."

"It is a *very* winning smile though." He grinned. "But you're right, I'd end up sleeping on the beach!"

"You'd need to find a good business partner, definitely." Josh sipped his drink. "Can Una and Noah recommend someone local?"

"I'm in no hurry to hang up my wings," Guy decided. "But this is paradise, isn't it? I get here whenever I can. I've been coming to St Seb's for nearly thirty years!"

Josh was relieved that Guy wasn't going to retire just yet, but a seed had settled in his mind. Guy was older than him, and if he retired to the Caribbean, Josh would still be Basingstoke, holding teamwork seminars with bored executives.

But he wouldn't think about that just now.

"So when did you first come here, then?" Josh asked. "Was it when you first started to fly with BA?"

"Long before that," he admitted. "Pa was with the RAF too and he used to talk about this paradise he'd once seen from the air, like it was a dream he'd had. I was a bit of an adventurer back in those days so I made it my business to find it, and when I did, I fell for the place! I think I was *maybe* twenty, just about."

Josh tried to imagine what twenty-year-old Guy Collingwood had looked like. No silver in his hair, his skin smooth, but his eyes would still have twinkled, Josh was sure of it. "Quite a place to come when you're twenty! And to be honest, when you're twenty-nine too." Josh lowered his voice, in case Guy's answer to his next question was a sad one. "Did your dad get the chance to come here too?"

"Once." He smiled and shook his head. "He hated it, not enough to do for a busy fellow like him. He always had to be *achieving*. To him, sitting here like this would be time wasted, time when he could be doing something useful. He couldn't see the value in just…this. Being still."

Had twenty-year-old Guy got on with his father? "Bet he was proud when you joined the RAF too."

"The first and last time." Guy shrugged. "I did a lot of things to make Pa proud—I even got married to make Pa proud—none of it worked, the marriage *certainly* didn't. Being gay though, that was the last straw. We were always very civilized, of course, but never exactly *close*. What about your folks?"

Josh smoothed the back of Guy's hand. *Married?* "Sorry you went through that. I can't imagine you being with a woman... What a tough situation." He scanned Guy's expression for a moment, before going on. "Me? Well, my parents are cool with it. My dad's sister married her girlfriend not long ago, and it was so nice seeing all the family there. Funny thing is, my mum said she's proud of me, but couldn't I do something a bit more *interesting* than HR! She reckons I should retrain as a teacher, but I dunno."

"I'm glad your parents are happy for you." Guy lifted Josh's hand and kissed it. "Because I don't want there to be any surprises when we're back in gray old England... I have a son and the divorce was a mess and — we haven't seen each other in a decade."

Josh felt a pang for Guy, for the confident man who, he now realized, wasn't as carefree as he first appeared. "*Fuck* — sorry. But, Guy...what a situation to end up in. You've got a son? I'm so sorry. Really. That must be so difficult for you."

"I did the typical absent dad thing," he admitted. "When work took me off, I threw money at him as if that was a substitute for asking my boy how school was going. And I realized that way, way too late."

"You're still his dad, though." Josh cupped Guy's face in his hand. The happy twinkle in his eyes was muted now. "You'll always be a part of him. Even if you haven't seen him."

"My dad wasn't there for me and I did the same thing to my own son." He closed his eyes for a moment. "I should've known better. I hope one day... Well, the phone might still ring."

Josh went back to his bun for a moment. He'd never had a boyfriend who was a dad before, and he wasn't quite sure what to say. But he'd done enough coaching in his time to suggest, "Or *his* phone might ring?"

"I wouldn't dare, because he might not answer." Guy took a sip from his glass. "If that changes anything for you, I really wouldn't blame you, darling."

"It doesn't change a thing." Josh smiled. "Okay, I'll admit I've never dated someone's dad before, but...that's cool. And if you want me to help you get back in touch with your son, somehow...if I can mediate or whatever, just say."

"That's all the skeletons in my particular cupboard." He smiled gently in reply. "Pretty standard middle-aged-ex-military-now-out stuff. I just wanted you to know who you're with."

"Thanks. For being honest. I really appreciate it, Guy." Josh brushed his fringe back from his face. "And I have to tell you that I don't have any children, and I'm not a poet or a pearl diver, but I *was* on my school's country dancing team and we *did* dance at the Hampshire County Fair. We came second — my mum's still got my medal and the photo from the newspaper. That's *my* skeleton!"

"You scandalous thing!" He laughed, his gaze lighting up again. "And I told you last night that I'm single, but honestly, I'd be very happy if that's no longer true. What do you say?"

Josh smiled awkwardly at Guy. "Boyfriends? Yeah, okay, why not?"

"God, I'm clumsy!" Guy pulled a comical grimace. "Out of practice and hopelessly dazzled by this gorgeous bloke I know!"

"Sorry — I'm just...I'm just amazed you like me so much!" Josh laughed. "Honestly. You're amazing, and I'm...well, I never thought I'd be the sort of person a handsome, dashing pilot would want to go out with. But I'm really glad I am!"

"You bowled me over," Guy admitted. "I blame that fringe, it's deadly!"

Josh let it fall over one eye and gave Guy a comical pout. "*And* for taking your bun! Admit it — you couldn't resist a man who has the same taste in pastries as you."

"But if you hadn't taken my bun, what would I've used as an excuse to talk to you?"

"Seriously?" Josh took Guy's hand again. "When did my fringe ensnare you, Captain Guy? I didn't see you until you spoke, and I turned, and…there was this insanely attractive pilot stood there behind me in the queue."

A faint flush colored Guy's cheeks as he admitted, "You were battling with your luggage tags just outside the duty free and you sort of…glanced up? And I thought, *bloody hell, he's gorgeous!*"

Josh blushed in sympathy with him. "I remember now… I was trying to put my shopping away. And realized I couldn't cram anything more into my bag! I saw someone in blue just out of the corner of my eye, and thought, *must be a pilot*, which isn't an unreasonable guess in an airport, but I couldn't see you properly — because of my fringe!"

"And then there you were, on *my* plane! So I sent Teri in to bat for me." Guy grinned.

"She must've worn a line in the carpet going backward and forward with our messages!"

"And when I managed a moment to see you, you were dead to the world!" He leaned forward and kissed Josh gently. "And still gorgeous."

"Shows what a smooth flight you're capable of." Josh tangled his fingers with Guy's and raised an eyebrow. "You have such clever hands."

"*Smooth.*" Guy nodded. "I'll take that."

"You're pretty smooth all round, I'd say!" Josh beamed. As if to prove the point, Captain Collingwood settled his hands on Josh's waist and scooped him out of his chair and into his own lap. The kiss that followed was just as smooth as Josh had said, but filled with heat too.

Josh caressed the triangle of Guy's chest that showed through the vee of his robe, then slipped his hand inside to Guy's nipples. He tweaked them softly and was fairly sure he could feel something start to press against him through Guy's robe. How he was going to be able to drag himself away later to meet Rey and all the others, he wasn't sure. But at least he'd be able to slip from the gathering for a rendezvous with Guy.

Guy's moan of pleasure sent a thrill through him and he felt his lover's hand in his hair, tangling softly. Concentrating on wedding rehearsals and polite conversation with the families was *not* going to be easy.

"Back to bed?" Josh loosened the belt on his robe. He wasn't going to risk full nudity on the balcony in daylight, but surely no one would mind an unfastened robe.

"Another moment?" Guy took the champagne from the ice bucket. "I'm all yours."

Chapter Five

Josh wasn't paying much attention as he stood on the jetty, waiting for the hotel's launch to arrive from the mainland.

He was still picturing Guy, wearing only his shorts, casually splashing his way down the steps from Josh's balcony and swimming back to his palace. His strong, tan back had looked so perfect against the blue sea and he had swum with his customary insouciant charm. Each stroke as he'd pulled himself through the water had seemed so easy, and Josh had watched him go, holding Guy's shirt against his cheek, left for him as a souvenir. The shirt Josh was wearing now as he waited on the jetty.

The roar of a speedboat interrupted Josh's thoughts, and he waved as the wedding party arrived.

There were the bride and groom, beaming and happy, four proud parents and a gaggle of assorted bridesmaids and relatives from both sides. Each looked as delighted as the next but Josh thought he saw just a hint of tightness in the face of Priscilla, the groom's mother, but maybe that was to be expected. Weddings seemed inordinately stressful at the best of times, without flying across the globe to tie the knot.

"Joshy!" Rey called, waving his hand. "Looking the part already! How's island life?"

"I am the most relaxed dude in the universe right now, Mr. Freddie *Rey* Reynolds!" Josh stood beside the hotel's bellboy, the waves lapping the pillars of the jetty below, and helped to lift the suitcases and bags from the boat. "Did you guys have a good flight?"

"Soon-to-be Mrs. Reynolds slept all the way here." Rey laughed, earning a nudge from Stella. "So I had a great time!"

"Oh, *Rey*!" Stella giggled. "Well, I don't want big circles under my eyes in the wedding photos!" She was a lovely woman, Josh had to admit. They would be very happy together, he was sure.

Josh leaned toward the boat, offering his hand to his friends as they climbed ashore. Martin, Rey's father, greeted him with a firm clap on the shoulder and beamed. "Hello, best man! How's that speech looking?"

"It was pretty short once I made it suitable for Pris' ears!" Josh grinned at Rey's mum. She'd always liked Josh's cheekiness, but not today apparently. Today she raised her sunglasses and narrowed her eyes at him. Sounding more serious now, Josh said, "Don't worry, I won't ruin the wedding, I promise."

Priscilla unpursed her lips for long enough to say, "You better not, Josh. There's sharks out to sea, and I'll be feeding you to them for their dinner if you're not careful."

Josh watched her as she climbed out onto the jetty in her impractical kitten-heeled shoes. Someone clearly wasn't coping with their jetlag.

Not like Guy.

"Didn't I tell you, Stella?" Rey snuggled his fiancée close. "It's paradise."

"It's so gorgeous! This sunshine is so lovely, and I'm so warm already, and I can't wait to get into the sea!" Stella twirled a length of her golden hair around her finger as she turned to Josh. "Although that'll have to wait until after the wedding, because I don't want to wreck my hair."

Josh wasn't sure how to tell her that not all gay men were obsessed with hairdressing, but he let it slide.

"Welcome to St Sebastian, everyone!" Josh said excitedly. "Do you want to get unpacked, then I can show you an amazing beach bar I found last night? It's brilliant!"

"Sounds like a plan!" Rey laughed, looking around. "What a place!"

"I'm not sure I'll be going to the beach bar," Priscilla decided. "I'll have a cocktail in the hotel bar, just us ladies! Mums, bride and bridesmaids."

"Behave," Martin teased. "I'm not paying to bail you lot out!"

Josh was two seconds away from asking Pris if she was going to join in with the limbo dancing advertised as that night's hotel entertainment, but he decided it was best avoided. "Rey, do you want me to come and help you unpack your groom uniform?"

"Yeah, with a few beers?" Rey patted Martin's arm and grinned at Stella's father. "See you in an hour, Dad? You two get a nap in pre-pub like proper old fellas?"

"Very subtle, Freddie." Martin shook his head. "We'll see you later."

The party broke up and Josh wheeled Rey's suitcase along behind him as they headed to the hotel.

"You'll *love* the beach bar," Josh told him. "And the view from the cabins is amazing—just beautiful ocean, as far as you can see. The sound of the waves is so relaxing! I *love* it here."

"Mum's not happy," Rey told him. "Let's hope paradise wins her over!"

"I thought it was jet lag." Josh winced. "Hope nothing goes wrong at the wedding, or maybe she really *will* feed me to the sharks!"

"It's the venue," he sighed. "It's way too depressing to go into. Let's get unpacked and get the beers in, yeah? Have a good time?"

On the way into the hotel, a beach vendor wandered up to them with a tray of jewelry. Josh would've walked past, but he stopped now to look at their wares. "Rey, why don't you get Stella a little present? I'm going to get something…"

Josh smiled at the vendor as he looked through the jewelry. He decided on two necklaces made from shells—not identical, as he chose one with blue and white shells for himself, and another with brown and cream for Guy. Complementary, rather than the same.

"Go on, Rey…choose something for the woman of your dreams!"

Rey paused, then selected a pretty shell bracelet in a rainbow of dazzling blues. As they walked on, he told Josh, "Did you see the dads? They've both been up since the crack—they're ready to drop where they stand!"

"No partying down the beach bar for them tonight!" Josh said.

He led Rey to the reception desk to check in. It was all admirably quick and staff were dispatched to show the members of the party to their rooms. Josh, feeling like an old hand by now, led Rey toward the little hut on stilts that was his for the night. And tomorrow, he'd be a married man.

"This is almost the same as my room!" Josh grinned. When his glance fell on the bed, he smiled to himself, remembering his night and morning with Guy. "There should be a couple of beers in your fridge..."

"I might need more than a couple." Rey opened the fridge and took out the beers. He tossed one over to Josh, who caught it. "I'm not going to lie, mate, I'm terrified! Groom's nerves, Dad reckons."

Josh popped open the tab on the can. "It's a big thing, isn't it? Marriage...committing to someone. And everyone wants it to be the perfect day, with nothing going wrong... It's a hell of a lot of pressure. But don't worry — I'm your best man and I will do everything I can to make your wedding run smoothly."

"And as we're getting on the plane this morning — that bloody weather report hasn't helped!"

Josh nearly choked on his beer. He wiped the foam away from his mouth. "Weather report? Sorry, I haven't heard anything about the weather — my phone's conked out. And I've been...busy."

"There's a tropical storm that might miss us. Or might hit us." He opened his can. "Depending on which weather forecast you read!"

"Oh, balls..." Josh tapped his finger against his can. "I noticed the wind picked up a bit last night, but it seemed really calm this morning. Let's hope it doesn't come anywhere near us!"

"Right, let's drink serious amounts of beer." He took a long, deep swig. "And celebrate my last night as a single Freddie!"

Josh put his arm around his friend's shoulder and clinked his beer against Rey's. "And no more wedding fears for Freddie Reynolds! You and Stella are great together, you make a lovely couple and I know you'll be happy forever and ever. Even when you're sitting side by side in front of the telly in your orthopedic reclining armchairs!"

"Where's this bar then?" Rey grinned. "We can drink this one as we walk."

"Follow me!" As they headed out of the hotel's grounds and onto the beach, Josh could see the bar up ahead. Maybe Guy would be there, and he could introduce Rey to him, but he didn't want to leap in and tell Rey, *I've met the most amazing bloke and with a fair wind I'll fall in love with him*, because now was time for Rey and Stella's romance.

He'd have to ask the plus-one question at some point. Maybe another beer down the line.

"I haven't been to St Sebastian since I was about ten," Rey confessed as they strolled. "And I'd remembered it as being perfect. And it is!"

Josh hadn't realized that Rey had been here before. He jabbed his thumb behind them, gesturing to their hotel. "Were you staying in the huts-on-stilts then too, or hadn't they been built then?"

"I stayed in a tent on the beach, and I had the time of my life." He shielded his eyes against the sun. "Best holiday ever."

"That sounds amazing! Wish I'd come here when I was ten." Josh pictured Priscilla's hairsprayed cloud of chestnut waves. "Bet your mum hated it, though. Where would she have plugged in her curling tongs in a tent?"

"Bless her." Rey sighed. "She wasn't here. I'll tell you later, if I get drunk enough!"

"That doesn't surprise me — she doesn't seem the tent type!" Josh led the way up to the bar and Noah greeted them. "This young man is about to get married. I prescribe the most ridiculous cocktails you have, with millions of paper umbrellas and plastic mermaids and sparklers. Don't you think so, Rey?"

"Bring it on," he agreed. Across the bar, Teri sat with a woman Josh now recognized as a fellow flight attendant. She spotted him and pantomimed a look of saucy shock, fanning her face with her hand. "Who's your lady friend?"

"Oh, that's Teri, she was the flight attendant on plane yesterday. That's the other flight attendant with her." Josh waved across the bar to her. "They're a really nice bunch."

And one person in particular…

"I would be if I had her job!" Rey waved and she raised her glass in reply.

"Yeah, it must be great to travel. Erm…I was going to ask — " Before Josh could pop in a mention of his plus one, Noah appeared with two cocktails that were just as ridiculous as Josh had hoped. He paid Noah, and he and Rey laughed as the sparklers fizzed. The drink inside the glass seemed to glow radioactively. "I am *so* getting flashbacks to Freshers' Week!"

"Oh God, don't remind me!" Rey winced. "Me and you unpacking our pots and pans in the kitchen and both trying to be dead cool. And bloody Mum saying, *'Go and introduce yourself, he looks like a nice boy!'"*

"Do you remember my awful plates? Those horrible stripy ones which I thought were the best thing ever?" Josh rolled his eyes. "And then we went to the Students' Union bar and got hammered and were doing karaoke before ten o'clock at night! But it was fun."

"And we both turned out all right, didn't we?" He took a sip of his drink. "That's bloody potent!"

Josh took a mouthful of his. "Bloody hell, how many bottles of rum is in *that*?" He stirred it, watching the colors change. "It's like drinking a lava lamp! Hey, look…I hope this doesn't seem really, really weird, and I'll stump up the dosh if needs be, but it'd be really awesome, and I'd be so grateful… Could I have a plus one for the reception? Would you mind?"

"Oh yes? Holiday romance?" He raised one eyebrow. "No problem. Is he coming to the ceremony too? Bit of moral support for the best man?"

"I wasn't sure if you'd want a stranger at the ceremony, but…if you wouldn't mind." Josh leaned closer, conspiratorial. "He's housetrained, I promise, and he's so handsome, all the bridesmaids and the mums will faint."

"Bloody hell, is he going to outdo the groom?" Rey grinned. "We're getting married on the beach—I think we'll end up with plenty of unexpected guests! Smart dress code though, no flip-flops!"

"Don't you worry about that. He can dress formal." Josh gave Rey a wink, then stirred his drink again. "I suppose it *is* a bit of a holiday romance. We only met yesterday. But…turns out he doesn't live that far away from me back in England, and we've decided to give it a go. Rey, I've got a boyfriend! Maybe it's this wedding, it's making me feel romantic!"

Rey smiled and told him, "That's what weddings do!"

"I know you'll probably think I'm being *way* over the top, but he's the sort of man I could fall in love with." Josh blushed and sipped his drink, his lips colliding with a tiny plastic palm tree clipped onto the rim of his glass. "I mean, I'm not in love with him yet, seeing as I only met him yesterday — that'd be ridiculous, wouldn't it — but he's just...just...*wonderful.*"

"Maybe it'll be your wedding next!" Rey took another slug of the drink, then told Noah, "Line up a couple more, please, mate!"

"Maybe it will, and you'll have to be *my* best man!" Josh nibbled the boozy slice of pineapple he'd found lurking in his drink. "Hang on...if there's two grooms, does that mean there's two best men? And what about bridesmaids? *Groomsmaids*, perhaps?"

"Take my advice. When you get married, just run off somewhere and do it. It's a bloody mare!"

Josh patted Rey's arm. "You sure you're okay? The storm might not come anywhere near here — they're unpredictable, you know."

"Mum's really pissed off," Rey admitted. "Because of the island."

"Why?" Josh glanced about the bar. All the customers were having a great time. He couldn't imagine what someone could have against the place. "St Sebastian is awesome! Unless she thought you were going to make her rough it under canvas?"

"Can I tell you something, mate? Without you thinking I'm a massive shit?"

There was something in Rey's tone that Josh wasn't too sure about. Something akin to a storm on the horizon. "Erm...yeah? You're not a massive shit, though, mate—we're best friends, right? You can tell me anything."

"I'm really, really scared about tomorrow." He glanced at Noah as he brought their drinks over, then addressed him. "Do you get a lot of weddings out here?"

Noah leaned against the bar with the air of a wiser older brother. "Yeah, we do. And I've seen more grooms than you can count come in here and look just as scared as you do right now." He gave Rey a matey slap on the arm. "Come on, man! Beautiful bride, handsome groom, what can go wrong?"

"Marriages can, can't they?" He was asking both men now. "Like, really wrong? Mum's first marriage — they ended up hating each other. What if *we* end up like them?"

"Her *first* marriage?" Josh blinked at Rey in surprise. "I'd never heard about that before. I mean, not that I'm an expert on my mates' parents or anything, but I didn't know she was married before she met your dad."

"Martin's my stepdad," Rey said, surprising Josh all over again. "But not really. He's been Dad since I was six. He's a stepdad, but he's *Dad* Dad."

The floor was suddenly unsteady under Josh's feet, as if it were laid on sliding sands. "He's your stepdad?" Josh took a large mouthful of his cocktail. Then he put the glass down and shook his head. "But that doesn't mean you and Stella will split up. You love each other, right?"

"We really, really do." He blinked, as though trying to focus. "I just keep thinking... What if we don't always? It's natural to worry, right?"

"You got to do what feels right," Noah advised sagely. "See that woman over there? That's Teri. We've been seeing each other some time. She flies over here, we spend a few days together, then she's gone back to England and we wait until she's here again. I'd marry her like that!" He snapped his fingers. "Maybe it'll happen one day. You're lucky, man. You've got a beautiful fiancée, right? She loves you, you love her. And maybe—one day, maybe you won't love each other anymore. But if you love her right now, why worry? Get that ring on her finger and you won't regret it."

Rey nodded slowly, as though it was the wisest thing he'd ever heard. "You should ask your Teri," he said. "Life's short."

Noah watched Teri from the corner of his eye. His smile was so gentle that Josh felt the floor shift beneath him again at the sight of so much love in Noah's expression.

"Maybe I should." He gave Teri a wink. She replied with a coquettish wave and mouthed, *love you*. Noah wandered over to her and took her hand.

"Oh, he's not, is he? Right here in the bar?" Josh stared, open-mouthed. "You've started everyone off, now, Rey! There won't be anyone single left on St Sebastian by the time you've finished!"

Teri was peering intently at Noah. She blinked then her eyes widened and she squealed, "Oh my God, yes!"

"She's keen!" Rey laughed finally and raised his glass. "Here's to them!"

Noah flung his arms around her and kissed her full on the mouth. Just then, a woman emerged from the kitchen, a tea towel in her hand. "Noah!"

He broke from the kiss and turned to her with a grin. "She says *yes*, Mum! Me and Teri are going to get married!"

"Una!" Teri clapped her hands together in excitement. "I did! I said yes!"

Una flung down the tea towel and hurried to the happy couple, embracing the two of them at the same time. "And now I need a new hat!"

"Do you think the Cap will give me away?" Teri clung to Una and Noah, tears shining in her eyes. "Can I ask him? He will, won't he?"

Una laughed. "Sure he would! You're the daughter he never had!"

Josh swallowed. There was something wrong with his eyes. Something obscuring them, hiding the scene before him.

Tears. Big, fat tears were rolling down his face, and he hugged Rey. "Mate, you and Stella will be great — Mr. and Mrs. Reynolds!"

Rey didn't answer but Josh knew why — he could feel his friend's tears on his shoulder.

"It's the booze." Rey eventually managed to laugh, over the happy sobs of Teri. "I'm wouldn't be crying without it!"

Josh squeezed Rey's shoulder. "It's okay to be scared! You're doing a really big thing. But it's going to be amazing, and Stella's just great, and I've hired a bloody tux!"

"I better not have another after this." Rey finally lifted his head and wiped his eyes. "Can't be slaughtered for the eve of the wedding dinner, Mum'd do her nut!"

"Shall I come with you to the hotel?" Josh brushed his fringe from his eyes. "But I might nip back here for a drink with Noah and Teri!"

"Just don't forget dinner at seven on the dot," Rey told him. "It's all got to be clockwork, or Stella and the mums'll panic. I promise we'll be done by ten, okay? I'm going to have a quick beer with the dads then get a few hours' kip—I feel like death warmed up."

"Don't worry, I won't miss the dinner," Josh promised. "Tell you what, you'll wish we were having dinner here, but I'm not sure I can see your mum getting over the beach in those heels!"

"She had trainers on the plane," he confided. "Went to the loo and came out all glammed up. She said she wants to do this in style!"

"I love your mum, and I love her enormous Joan Collins clip-on earrings!" Josh raised his glass. "To Pris! And to Martin! And to Stella…and most especially to *you*, dear old Rey-Rey the Reymeister!" Josh blinked. What the hell was in this cocktail to make him sound like an annoying undergrad again?

"She had her ears pierced in honor of the wedding!" Rey let out a long-suffering sigh. "Stella and Mum went to a spa and she came back with her ears pierced. She was all, '*I went wild! I've got piercings!*'"

"Christ, I bet you panicked for a moment!" Josh chortled and slapped his hand down on the bar. "Sorry, mate. But see…weddings make people do weird things!"

"Especially mums!"

"Just as long as she doesn't really try to feed me to the sharks, we should all be okay!" Josh clinked his glass against Rey's. Rey laughed and slumped happily against the bar, as though an invisible thread holding him upright had been snipped. He looked like a different man already, relaxed or just knackered.

"Cap?" Teri's voice was loud with excitement as she positively shouted into her phone. *Cap.* Josh couldn't help but smile, because Guy was currently getting his ear blasted somewhere in the island. "Can I come and see you? Yes, he's here!"

She glanced at Josh and mouthed, *he says hello.* "I'll be five minutes!"

Hello! Josh mouthed in return, accompanied by a camp wave.

"He says hello back," he heard her say. Then she pocketed her phone and, dragging Noah with her, approached the bar. Leaving her fiancé to go back to his customers, Teri whispered to Josh as she passed, "The boss' having a beach day at cabana." She arched a *very* saucy eyebrow. "Just so you know."

With that promise of Guy reclining on a beach in the sun and, Josh realized, probably wearing very little indeed, Teri was gone. Rey watched her as she wandered away along the beach, then decided, "It's all happening here!"

"I've only been here a day, but I'm convinced this place is magical." Josh took the pair of necklaces he'd bought from the beach vendor out of their paper bag and put both on. He winked at Rey. "One for me, one for the boyfriend — when I see him later."

"How much're you enjoying saying *my boyfriend*?" Rey grinned. "He's a lucky guy, I hope he knows that!"

Lucky Guy indeed!

"I dunno, I'm the lucky one, really — he's amazing." Josh had to pull himself out of a daydream where Guy was enjoying his *beach day* wearing nothing but factor 50 and a smile. "We're going to make a go of it, back in England. I really hope it works out. I *have* told him I'm just an HR manager, but he doesn't seem to mind!"

"Well, I can't wait to meet him." His friend gave a drunken smile and adopted a rather comical snooty air. *"I hope your intentions toward my awesome mate are honorable, sir!"*

"They are very dishonorable indeed, sir, and I'm all for it!" Josh quipped.

"Right." Rey downed his drink and took a deep breath. "Let's find the dads, try and sober up a bit, then have a last-minute panic about whatever the mums are freaking out over today. Ready?"

Josh patted Rey's shoulder. "Ready."

Chapter Six

Priscilla was hardly the most relaxed of people, but as Josh watched her order everyone into the hotel's breakfast room, where she then arranged the wedding party around the stacked tables and chairs, Josh did his best to give Rey a reassuring wink.

"She'll be fine, everything'll be fine." Josh sincerely hoped it would be. It didn't look it though. In fact only Martin, Rey's dad — stepdad as he now knew — looked anything like relaxed. In fact, it seemed to be his default setting.

"She's not letting Stella's mum get a look in," Rey muttered, folding his arms. "It's embarrassing. I'll be the one who gets it in the neck from Stel when we're on our own."

"Stella's mum is a grown woman — she can have a word with your mum if she wants to. She doesn't look *too* unhappy." Although she certainly didn't look all that pleased, that was for sure.

"I thought I told you to pay to attention!" Priscilla sighed, hands on her hips. "You two boys, honestly —

we've got a wedding tomorrow. This is our last chance to rehearse! And. We're. Going. To. Get. It. Right!"

Pierre, the minister, the most chill person in the room, strolled toward Priscilla. Weddings evidently held no fear for him. "Mrs. Reynolds, we'll get it right — if you stand just over here, with Mr. Reynolds?"

He gestured toward the space next to Martin. Then he looked up toward the end of the room. "And Stella, you ready at the back with your dad? Give me a thumbs up!"

"What about Mum?" Stella called, nodding to where her own mother waited beside the door, her lips set in a tight line. "She's completely not part of any of this and she's the bride's mum. It's like she's not here!"

Josh looked down at his hands. Stella sounded as annoyed as Angie looked. *Like daughter, like mother.*

"I'm just here to hold the door," Angie said coolly. "Apparently."

"Bride's mother?" Martin shook his head. "Star of the show back where I come from. Get yourself onto this pretend front row, Ang, this wedding can't happen without you in pride of place. Come on. Sure, you can't leave me to deal with Pris' perfume on my own, now!"

A tight laugh ran through the wedding party. Priscilla even managed a grimace. "I just...my son's wedding... I just want it to go well."

She looked at Martin, her large eyes edged with worry, and Josh swallowed. As annoying as Priscilla was in mother-of-the-groom mode, Josh could appreciate why she was being like this. If her marriage to Rey's dad hadn't worked out, then her need to make this perfect for Rey was even more acute. Almost as if she was trying to make it up to him. But Josh couldn't bring it up, so he patted Rey's arm.

"We all want it to go well," Angie told her as she took her place beside Pris. She offered her opposite number a very sympathetic smile and added, "Because you and me will never hear the end of it if it doesn't."

"It's going to go well!" Stella informed everyone in a razor-sharp voice, so sharp that Rey started a little. "Except, oh, we've just been talking in reception about a tropical *bloody* storm that might be heading right for us, yay, go me! Wedding day hurricane incoming!"

Pierre headed up the imaginary aisle toward Stella, an avuncular smile on his face. "We get storm warnings all the time, and most of them never touch us. And if they do, we get a little bit of rain and a little bit of wind. And that's all. So…big smile for the minister? And bridesmaids too?"

Pierre looked around Stella and counted. Josh counted as well.

Oh, shit.

"Rey, how many bridesmaids should there be, versus how many are actually standing behind your lovely fiancée at this moment?"

"For fuck's sake—" Rey clamped his hand over his mouth. "Sorry, Reverend, sorry, Mum. Sorry, everybody else, but… Did anyone see Louise? Wasn't she here like five minutes ago?"

Stella's eyes opened very wide and so did Pris', finally followed by Angie's. And for some reason, they all looked at Josh.

Josh pointed at himself and stared back at them. "She was here. Definitely. She was talking to one of the waiters outside. She—"

So I'm not the only wedding guest enjoying a holiday fling?

"Erm…has anyone seen that waiter? You know, the tall one with the bleached bit of hair just here?" Josh tugged at his fringe.

Priscilla glared. "You mean Louise has gone…gone AWOL with a waiter?"

"That's my nephew you're talking about!" Pierre remarked with a flash of roguish glee that had Josh trying to hide a splutter of laughter. What he wouldn't give to be with Guy now, sitting out on the veranda listening to the crashing waves, sipping ti' punch in the sunshine. Instead he was here, in what seemed to be the most stressful place in the Caribbean.

"Waiter…" Stella murmured, as though trying to remember something. Then her hand flew up to her mouth and she gasped, "Oh no. No way, no! Pris, you remember this morning when we in the airport bistro and I took out my wedding garter to show you and the waiter came up and interrupted—"

Priscilla's mouth fell open as if she was preparing to swallow a world-beating gobstopper. She wheeled round to face Stella. "And you've left in the café?"

"I put it on the chair, didn't I? Because you told me to, you and Mum were all, *don't let another man see your wedding garter*, and I put it on the chair and—" She took a deep breath and howled, "Why didn't one of you two tell me I'd not picked it up again? I'm getting married, I can't be expected to remember! It's still on the fucking chair at Heathrow!"

"It's not our job," Angie told her daughter. "We had enough on keeping your bridesmaids in one place. And look how that's ended up!"

"Someone probably handed it in," Rey ventured. The dads stayed resolutely silent, Josh noted. No doubt experience had taught them it was the best way. "We can pick it up on our way back through?"

"Erm... Rey..." Josh nudged him. "You know that rhyme, the one — "

Priscilla's stentorian tones erupted with, "The one that goes, *Something old, something new, something borrowed, something blue*?" In her voice, the old rhyme sounded like the words of a wizard bellowed through a storm at the stone door of a mountain to demand entrance.

"Something left on a chair at Heathrow," Rey finished, clearly hoping that levity was going to win the day. Josh already knew it wasn't. The air seemed to seethe, then, in the deepening silence, Martin cleared his throat.

"Reverend, correct me if I'm wrong, but am I right in thinking that there's no law saying a bride can't still have the best day of her life *without* something blue?" He gave a bright smile toward Pierre. "So really, the lost garter's nothing to commit murder over, is that not so?"

Pierre gave the most Gallic of Gallic shrugs. "Guadeloupe is a French territory, and we don't have a rhyme about weddings and *les objets bleus*." He smiled at Stella. "*Tant pis, ma petite!*"

Her face, which had been set in abject misery, was unmoving for a moment. Then she met Pierre's gaze and smiled. A small, rather wobbly smile, but a smile. Teri was lucky. Pierre seemed like the sort of father-in-law to have in one's corner.

"Can we do our rehearsal without a bridesmaid?" she asked, sniffing. "She'll be here tomorrow, I promise."

"So long as the vicar's nephew doesn't keep her out all night," Angie muttered to Pris.

"What does she think this is, a holiday?" Priscilla remarked.

Pierre smiled his benevolent smile again. "The other two can hold her up! But don't worry, I'll get my sister round to see my nephew, and you'll have a well-rested bridesmaid for tomorrow."

Rey nudged Josh and whispered, "I wish I'd met a waiter, then I wouldn't have to be at a wedding rehearsal."

'When you get married, just run off somewhere and do it,' Rey had told him earlier. It was beginning to seem like the most attractive option. *Running off somewhere with Guy... He's just* made *for romance.*

"It's a bit late to come out now!" Josh joked. Then he heard voices at the back of the room. Louise had returned. Stella, Pris and Angie all locked eyes with her as one. Each appeared more furious than the other, but nobody seemed more furious than Stella.

"Oh, so you decided to drop in?" Stella called to her. "That's really generous, Lou, thanks."

Louise appeared to be about to speak, but evidently changed her mind. "Sorry," she said in a small voice.

"Sorry," Stella repeated, but it sounded like a gunshot. She and Pris exchanged a glance and even though nothing was said, Josh saw an understanding pass between the two women. They were both furious with the wandering bridesmaid and she was about to get it with both barrels.

"*Sorry?*" Priscilla swung her arms like a sergeant major on the parade ground as she stabbed her heels over the carpet toward Louise. She poked her finger at Louise. "*Sorry?* You held up the wedding rehearsal to cavort with a waiter, and all you have to say for yourself is *sorry?*"

Josh had not, until that moment, ever seen someone take a step backward, but Louise now did.

Pierre interceded and threw a glance Martin's way. "Ladies… We're all here now, that's all that matters." He gave Louise a wink. "And my nephew's a handsome boy!"

And somehow, Josh just knew that wasn't the most helpful thing to say.

"But he'll still be handsome tomorrow — my wedding day only gets one chance to be spectacular!" Stella took her place beside Pris and Angie. The mother of the bride, who had felt so much like a spare part, was now suddenly very much part of the group. She completed the trio, the most fearsome girl band line-up Josh could imagine.

"From now on, bridesmaids are on curfew," Angie decided, earning decisive nods from Stella and Pris. "You can do what you like after the reception but until then, behave."

"Or I'll send Pris after you." Martin smiled, his efforts to lighten the atmosphere doing little to lift the look of annoyance from his wife's face.

Priscilla turned on him, her teeth bared like an Amazon warrior's. "Do you want to be fed to the sharks, Martin? Do you? And you two boys at the front there, don't think I can't see the smirks on your faces! Shark food, the lot of you!"

Josh's lips trembled with the force of the nervous giggle he was trying to restrain.

"Curfew?" Louise looked wounded. "But you said this was going to be a fun holiday! And I wasn't cavorting with anyone. I was only having a chat with Vadim. I've said sorry. I'm not at flipping school anymore."

"We can *all* have fun *after* the wedding," Stella told her, tears gathering in her eyes again. "You can do whatever you like then!"

Rey lifted his hand to his mouth to stifle a very theatrical cough and whispered to Josh, "*Heil, mein Führer.*" Then he dropped his hand and said, "Come on, Stel, let's get rehearsed so we can get to dinner. Everyone's a bit tired and…" He took a deep breath and Josh remembered his tears earlier that day, the wobble that this whole mess couldn't be helping. "Look, can we just get through it?"

"Well, now we're all here —" Priscilla glared at Louise again, then her look softened. "Let's get to it, chaps!"

"We're going to have an amazing day tomorrow," Rey told them all, dashing the back of his hand over his eyes. "And we're all knackered, let's be honest. You don't get much leg room in cattle class!"

Josh joined in their laughter, but thought of Guy and his first-class upgrade. *Leg room? I had my own bed!*

Pierre nodded. "Ready, everyone? Let's rehearse!"

How Pierre put up with wedding parties, Josh couldn't imagine. Even once this one was on track, it still seemed more like a military operation than a chance for two people to show the world that they loved each other, that they wanted to spend their lives together. Between Robbie Williams at the start and Beyoncé at the end, it was pageantry, poetic vows and expensive frocks, and all of it drilled to the nth degree until the romance sort of just…evaporated. But they loved each other, Josh knew that without a shadow of a doubt. Rey and Stella were the perfect couple, the most in tune pair he'd ever seen until — until he'd met Captain Guy Collingwood.

Sensible Josh would have listened wide-eyed to tales of the HR manager who met a pilot and fell head over heels with him beneath the Caribbean sun, but sensible Josh appeared not to have boarded the plane after all. The Josh who'd come to St Seb's was subtly different, as though the heat had melted his reserve and left him ready for romance. Ready for love, even.

But was Guy ready for that too?

Was he even looking for love, with that horrendous failure of a marriage in his past?

England would tell, Josh knew. In the deer park and the leaves, the pub and the vintage car, they'd still be Guy and Josh, just as they were on the beach of St Seb's. And if sensible Josh was waiting in Basingstoke to tell him this was all a ridiculous fancy, he'd tell sensible Josh where to get off. He was enjoying life with his dashing captain, and —

"Rings, mate," Rey said, nudging him. His hand was held out expectantly, for the imaginary rings. He really *was* taking rehearsals seriously. "You're miles away!"

"So're we all," Martin told them through a yawn. "I'll be for my bed before I get my pudding tonight! How about we shift our big dinner to the night after the nuptials? We'll all be a lot less strung out then, I reckon!"

"But we have to have a pre-wedding dinner!" Even as she said this, Priscilla stifled a yawn and slipped one foot out of its kitten-heeled shoe to rub her toes. "But...it *has* been a long day."

"I'm happy to put it off," Angie said, her husband giving one of his stoic, wordless nods. "Stella?"

Say yes, Josh thought. Because time not spent at what was sure to be a tense dinner was time he could spend with Guy.

"I'm shattered." Stella nodded. "Let's finish rehearsal, have a drink and just chill?"

"That's the best way to prepare for the wedding!" Pierre agreed. "You were all amazing, and all you need now is a good night's sleep."

Josh was fairly sure this was aimed at Louise, who might be tempted to break curfew, but it might just as well refer to Josh. But where better to sleep than in Captain Collingwood's bed?

Chapter Seven

Josh tried not to look pleased about the dinner being canceled, although the rest of the wedding party were probably too frazzled to notice. He yawned and mumbled something about jetlag, then went off to his room.

Josh dashed up the stairs to his hut, and nearly cheered at the sight of the phone charger waiting for him on the dressing table. He plugged it in and turned his phone on. It seemed like a miracle when the screen powered up, and he nearly cheered again when he saw that he had no fewer than three messages on his phone. *All from Guy.*

The first was last night's invitation to the island birthday party, the second a photo of the sparkling headland waters where Josh had swum before he knew Guy was staying in the palace. The photo had been taken that afternoon, as Josh had been rehearsing the wedding of the century, his mind occupied by thoughts of his dashing pilot. Accompanying the picture, his lover had typed, *What would make this picture perfect? xxxxx*.

The third and final text had been sent just ten minutes ago. No photo, no invitation, just three words.

I want you.

Josh almost dropped his phone. The room seemed alive with the memories of last night and he took a deep breath before tapping out his reply.

I want you too. Are you alone?

The reply landed in seconds.

Just me and the beach and a very nice bottle.

Josh pulled his shirt off over his head and chucked it aside.

I'm on my way.

And he heard the reply in that smooth voice.

I'll be waiting. Xxxxx

Josh changed into his swimming shorts, but just as he was about to head onto the balcony, realized that it wasn't a good idea to leave his phone charging in a wooden hut while he wasn't around. He unplugged it and turned the phone off. Then he went onto the balcony, locked the door behind him and stowed the key in his zip-up pocket.

He climbed into the water and swam along the line of the beach, which was lit with the lights from the bars and hotels. The water was warm, but Josh didn't dawdle. He powered through the waves and was soon rounding the headland. His heart pounded, not with the effort of his swim but with anticipation of seeing his captain again.

Josh could see Guy, he was sure of it, out on the veranda. He trod water for a moment. He'd spent his whole life being prudent, but the romance of St Sebastian had fired his blood. What if…what if on St Sebastian, HR managers could rise out of the water like Aphrodite?

Before he could tell himself not to, Josh slipped out of his shorts and bunched them up into one hand. Then he swam the rest of the way, wondering if Guy had spotted him yet.

He saw the moment that it happened. Standing there with his hands on the rail that ran around the veranda, the billowing white shirt he wore almost luminous in the moonlight, Guy leaned forward just a little to peer more closely at the ocean. Then he jogged down onto the beach, greeting Josh with a sweeping wave.

Josh dropped his feet down onto the sand below him and pushed his way through the water.

"Guy!" He grinned as he tried to hurry toward him. "I've been thinking about you all day!"

Josh slicked back his fringe and as the waves withdrew he rose from the water, naked but for a pair of shell necklaces. He held out his arms and grinned.

"Your very own Aphrodite pearl-diving poet is here!"

"Now *that* is how to make an entrance!" On the edge of the shore, Guy threw his arms around Josh and hugged him. Then he put his hands on Josh's face and kissed him as though they'd been parted for weeks, the sort of kiss a sensible fellow like Josh hadn't usually received from his past, equally sensible, boyfriends.

Josh responded, his kiss fiery and passionate. He pressed his wet body against Guy, holding himself close as he caressed his behind. "I'm glad you're alone tonight, because now I'm here."

"Come to bed?" Guy murmured, the stirring hardness in his cargo shorts pressing to Josh's naked skin. "You gorgeous bloody thing."

Josh grinned. "Lead the way, Captain!"

And just as he had last night, Guy fulfilled his dashing side of the deal, scooping Josh up into his arms and carrying him across the moonlit sand. Josh removed one of his necklaces and put it around Guy's neck. His gift to him—Josh's attempt at romance. Together they stepped up onto the veranda and through the billowing gauze curtains into the palace.

Bloody hell.

Captain Collingwood *did* have a four poster in his room. And a vast, gleaming bath, and a view of the beach stretched out before him.

But the only view he seemed interested in was the man in his arms.

Guy laid Josh on the crisp white sheets and knelt beside him for just as long as it took to sweep his shirt over his head and throw it aside. Then he took Josh in his arms again and kissed him, long and lingering. Josh combed through Guy's hair and caressed his handsome face, then drew his fingertips down Guy's back, kissing him all the while. But this wasn't only lust. It was more than that—it was a chance at love.

"Will you…" Josh wondered if he should say what was hovering on his lips, but somehow, Guy didn't seem to be the sort of man to find it ridiculous. "Don't laugh, but… Guy, will you make love to me?"

"Why would you think I'd laugh at that?" Guy touched his forehead to Josh's. "I'd love to make love to you."

Josh giggled awkwardly. He'd never asked anyone that before. "Your merman Ursula Andress, being demanding."

"I like that kind of demanding." He kissed Josh again. "Though I can't picture you in a bikini."

"Nothing but a necklace made of shells is much better!" As Josh looked up at Guy's bright blue eyes, he slid his hand down to Guy's shorts and slowly unfastened them. "That's all you should wear, too."

"I'll never take it off." Guy dipped his head to trail kisses over Josh's throat and told him, "You made a stunning Aphrodite."

"I've never done that before." Josh pushed Guy's shorts off him. He had at least done *that* before. "It was fun. I should do things like that more often, don't you think? As long as it's *your* beach I turn up on."

"Life's too short not to have fun. Even in Basingstoke."

"Not much opportunity to go about naked in Basingstoke, I'm sad to say. St Seb's is *much* better. Especially because…." Josh gave Guy a wink as he closed his hand around his erection and began to caress him. "Because you and your fantastic bod are here."

"Me and my fantastic bod," Guy said with a mischievous smile. "And yet I've never been to Basingstoke. Naked or otherwise."

"You'll have to visit. My bedroom's got a nice view of the canal…" Josh kissed him. "But we'll have to draw the curtains."

Guy lifted his head and peered at Josh, humor sparkling in his eyes. "You really are *terribly* sensible, aren't you? A nice view's there be enjoyed, as the narrowboaters would no doubt tell you. Not sure it'd have quite the same impact though, rising naked out of the canal with a shell necklace."

"With a duck balancing on my head?" Josh ran his free hand over Guy's broad chest. "I like St Seb's. I'm not all that sensible here… You haven't drawn *your* curtains and I've only just noticed!"

Guy's only reply this time was to kiss him again. He slid his fingertips lightly down Josh's side, caressing his skin until he curled his fingers around Josh's erection. Then he whispered, "St Seb's isn't a sensible sort of place."

"I'd noticed…" Josh's words ended in a sigh of pleasure. Sensible Josh would never have lain on clean sheets while leaving sand to fall out of his wet hair into the pillow. But sensible Josh had never asked a man to make love to him before, especially not a man he'd only met the day before. Josh crossed his legs around Guy's waist, bringing him closer to him.

"I'm sensible when it matters," Guy murmured against Josh's lips. Josh felt Guy's arm reach away from him and vaguely heard the sound of a drawer opening, seemingly as far away as the waves that were lapping at the shore outside. 'Sensible when it matters' felt like a very Guy way to be. It was perfect for St Seb's.

Josh tweaked Guy's nipple, toying with it as Guy prepared himself. Was there nothing could do without seeming so easy and assured? Evidently not.

Although last night had been so heated, tonight Josh felt something else, a distant thrumming of *something* that sensible Josh wouldn't recognize. He was drawn to Guy in a way he couldn't explain and didn't want to.

"I need you, Captain Collingwood," Josh murmured as he kissed Guy's neck. He heard his lover's answering sigh as Guy's free hand closed over his hip, lifting him just a little from the bed before Josh felt the tip of his erection teasing against him. Josh tightened his legs around him and moaned against Guy's neck as their bodies were united.

"I could fall in love with you," Josh admitted. But those were the words of sensible Josh, and he didn't belong here on St Seb's. "I mean... I think I already am falling in love with you."

"The island where magic happens," Guy breathed, catching Josh's earlobe lightly between his teeth for a second. "Let's bring some of it home to England?"

Josh was fairly sure that St Seb's magic followed Guy wherever he went, but Josh would bottle it somehow and stow it in his suitcase when he went home. His answer was to move his hips against Guy's, a soft moan in his throat at the sensation of being so close to the man who had, without asking, made Josh chuck his staid, prudent self aside. And where better to chuck it all aside than in this vast bed, the ocean stretched out before them and Guy Collingwood in his embrace? If a man was going to discover his romantic side, this seemed like this best place to do it.

Josh's body moved with Guy's as if they were already part of each other. Pleasure traveled through Josh, building and building, but so gently, unlike the passion of the night before. Josh gazed up at Guy, drawn to the sparkle of his blue eyes, to the desire and…was it love that Josh saw there? Affection, at least.

Are you falling for me too?

Guy's hand grew tighter around Josh's erection and as his hips moved harder, his kisses grew deeper too. The seashell around Guy's neck brushed against Josh's throat, as cool as their embraces were heated, and as Guy brushed a trail of kisses over Josh's jaw toward his ear, he heard that smooth, wonderful voice whisper, "We don't have to leave what we've got here on the island. We can take the magic home."

"I'd like that," Josh replied, his voice thick with pleasure. He stroked Guy's strong back in circles, thrilling at the pull and thrust of the muscles as Guy moved above him. What he would have expected from a man who had just celebrated his forty-ninth birthday Josh wasn't sure, but it wasn't this irresistible mixture of strength and romance, topped off with the sort of eyes that seemed to shine just for him. They *could* take this home, and they could make the English winter as hot as St Sebastian.

Josh pictured Guy at the wheel of his car, with a scarf wrapped around his neck, the branches of the bare wintry trees laced overhead as he drove through the country lanes. Guy would look just as handsome as he did in his loose cotton shirt—just as handsome as he did now, wearing only a necklace and a subtle sheen of sweat.

Josh slid his hands down to Guy's buttocks, cupping them as he thrust against him, wanting to feel Guy as deep inside him as he could be. His head tipped back on the pillow, his heart pounding, Josh panted Guy's name. He heard his own name gasped in reply, then Guy's mouth was on his neck, kissing and nuzzling, his hand moving harder and faster around Josh's erection. He *was* falling in love, and it felt glorious.

And it'd had never happened before. Not to Josh. His blood seemed to fizz inside him, a strange blend of excitement and comfort washing through him.

This wasn't sensible at all.

The tensing of Guy's muscles as his orgasm began to overtake him sent a fresh thrill through his body, a wonderful pull of desire for the man who shared his pleasure. Guy slipped his arm around Josh's shoulders, holding their bodies close together as they approached the edge.

Josh moaned, his whole body trembling as his climax took him. He'd never felt anything so intense before, and he held on to Guy as tightly as he could, as if all their desire and love could've washed them both away. Guy sank down onto him, his orgasm playing out in smaller thrusts, his breath hoarse against Josh's skin when he gasped, "You really are something."

Josh combed Guy's messy hair, covering his face in small kisses. "*You* are. I've never..." *Felt anything so intense before.* Josh held back. He'd terrify the man if he wasn't careful. "I've never made love with the curtains open."

"Is that some wonderfully filthy slang that I'm too old to understand?" Guy lifted his head a little and winked. "Or are you really *that* sensible?"

"I'm...I'm really that sensible." *Or I was, at least.*

"Maybe some of it'll rub off on me." Guy rolled onto the bed beside him. "But I suspect it's too late for that. You'll have to be the sensible one for both us. Or maybe I'll make you as silly as I am instead."

"Sounds like a good swap." Josh kissed the tip of Guy's nose, then rolled onto his side to admire him.

That broad chest.

"I want to know all about Josh." Guy smiled, studying his face. "What makes you happiest?"

Josh sighed. "If you'd asked me that a couple of months ago, I would've said a tidy desk and nice meal out. But seeing as you're asking me *now...*" Josh grinned at Guy and tweaked his nipple. "I'd say lying in a huge bed on a tropical island with a handsome man called Guy."

"Oh well, that's very fortunate." He grinned, then gave a very contented sigh. "I don't usually look forward to leaving St Seb's, but this time, England's going to seem a lot more appealing. Autumn leaves and my man waiting for me. Perfect."

My man. Josh smiled.

"There's a lovely pub I want to take you to." Josh propped himself up on one arm and kissed Guy's forehead. "You could always drive us in that car of yours. It's really old, out in the countryside, and it's got a huge old fireplace, and it's lovely to go there on a cold day and feel all warm and... Sorry, I suppose I should say, *there's this club I go to with ear-splittingly loud music and I go there every weekend and dance till dawn.* But I prefer the pub. There's even a pub cat."

"I'd like a little cat." Guy pouted. "But they won't let them on the flight deck. Your pub sounds perfect, just the place for an old rogue to squire his glorious boyfriend, don't you think?"

"Oh yes, definitely." A cat. Josh could picture one nestled on Guy's knee. "Tell me...about this car of yours. Do you wear a cravat when you drive it? I dunno... maybe it's the RAF thing, but...I reckon you'd suit a cravat."

"I've probably got one somewhere. It feels like something I *would* have." He narrowed his eyes, as though trying to remember if there was a cravat somewhere in a drawer in Farnham just waiting to be rediscovered. "But the car I *can* bore you witless with. She's stunning, Josh, perfect condition just as she was when she rolled off the line all those years back. You're going to love her." Guy fell silent then blinked and Josh saw the barest hit of a flush creeping over his cheeks. He grinned and admitted, "Car bore, darling, sorry."

Josh tickled Guy's chest. "Oh, shush — you must know that everything you say in that sexy voice of yours sounds amazing."

"My voice?" He laughed, but the flush didn't deepen. *He knows.* "I have no idea what you mean."

Josh tried to deepen his voice and murmured, in his best attempt at Guy's buttery tones, "Ladies and gentlemen, this is your captain speaking. We're not flying anywhere today because Josh won't let me leave the bed. We'll be having lots and lots of lovely sex."

"Ladies and gentlemen, *this* is your captain speaking," Guy purred, pressing his lips to Josh's shoulder. "Can I interest you in a glass of champagne and the best bath on the island?"

That voice. At those mellow tones, Josh's body was already reviving. How embarrassing, to be so keen.

"How can I say no to that? First class is getting ever more luxurious, Captain Collingwood!"

"Give me two minutes and I'll be with you." Guy winked. "Why don't you get the bath running?"

Josh kissed him before getting up from the bed. Guy followed and, utterly confident in his nudity, strolled through into the en suite. Josh was left in the bedroom, bathed in moonlight.

Josh went over to the bath by the bedroom window and sat on its edge. He lazily swirled his hand through the rising water. Paradise seemed to get better and better.

"I'm going to make a naked champagne run," Guy told him as he wandered back into the bedroom. "Wish me luck!"

Guy, naked, with champagne? Josh chuckled to himself as he chose a bubble bath for them and poured in a generous splash. He breathed in the aroma, taking a deep breath of that exotic scent as Guy slipped back into the room.

"Champagne," he announced, holding up a bottle and two glasses. "For me and my glorious boyfriend."

"Now there's a welcome sight!" Josh dipped his hand into the bath. "And the water's just right."

"So, tell me…" Guy set the glasses down on the edge of the bath and tore the foil from the neck of the bottle. "Whose HR do you manage?"

Josh held the stems of the glasses. "An IT services firm that I doubt you'll have heard of. It's…well, it's a job."

"You sound terribly enthusiastic." He took hold of the cork and, with a loud *pop*, opened the champagne. "No pre-wedding jitters, I hope?"

"None for me, no. Can't say I know how the others are coping!" Josh watched as Guy filled the glasses. "I suspect I'm having the most fun, though."

"God, the night before my wedding…" Guy grimaced and put the bottle down. It couldn't have been much worse than the rehearsal Josh had just endured, but it didn't feel like the moment to bring up missing garters and runaway bridesmaids. "I flew Tornados in the Balkans and even *that* didn't worry me as much as getting married. It's so different now, everyone's a lot less hung up on who we want to sleep with, thank God."

Josh took Guy's hand. "It was very brave of you — the Tornados *and* the wedding. I wouldn't have the foggiest idea what to do if I found myself married to a woman! But you *definitely* know what to with a man."

"So I pass muster?" Guy climbed into the bath and helped Josh over the edge, a gentleman through and through. The water was wonderfully warm, the bubbles covering its surface. "I wasn't brave for getting married. I was a coward. But I'm not the sort of chap who does angst. It takes far too much effort!"

Josh sat down in front of Guy and leaned back against his chest. "Like you said, it was different then. You...you did what you had to do." Josh kissed Guy's hand, then picked up his champagne. "A toast to us — to the future?"

"To our future?" Guy reached for his champagne. "Guy and Josh? *Gosh*?"

"To Gosh!" Josh laughed and clinked his glass against Guy's. "We have a portmanteau name? That's *awesome!*"

"It was too perfect *not* to use." Guy reached his arm around Josh's waist and let his hand rest against his thigh beneath the bubbles. "We see a lot of weddings on the island, but none of them have a best man as gorgeous as you. I hope they know how lucky they are."

"At least there's no chance of me running off with the bride!" Josh brushed his hand over Guy's where it lay against his leg. "*I'm* lucky, really. I've never traveled so far away from home. I almost turned Rey down when he asked me to be best man, but... I'd always wanted to travel. I never got round to it. Everyone else spent their gap year backpacking around Australia, and what did I do? Got a job on the tills in Tesco's. Saved up for uni, you see. Very sensible. Then I was saving up for my flat, so although I kept Googling holidays in Thailand, I never went. So when Rey asked, I thought, *Why not? What else are interest-free credit cards for?* And now I'm here, I'm so bloody glad I told sensible Josh to shove off and let me have some fun!"

"That's the spirit," Guy agreed. "So is Thailand your dream destination? Or was it just a case of anywhere that isn't England?"

"It had nice beaches when I looked!" Josh gestured outside to the beach, which had been rapidly consumed by the night. "Maybe I'll go there one day. I don't know. It just looked quite different from where I used to go on holiday when I was a child. And by the way... I didn't mention the credit card thing to ask for a handout. I'll have it paid off in a couple of months. Oh hell... Am I being awkward?"

"Darling, I didn't think you had, don't worry." Guy's lips brushed another kiss to the nape of Josh's neck. "If you fancy Thailand, we'll go to Thailand. We'll go anywhere you like. It's a perk of being friendly with the flight deck."

"That would be so amazing. But you know, I'd go anywhere with you, Guy." Josh sipped his champagne. "Even one of those Father Christmas reindeer rides in Lapland!"

"Oh, I'd love to do that! A real sleigh ride?" He stroked Josh's thigh. "If you've never seen the northern lights, we have to do that together. I remember the first time I saw them from the flight deck. It was one of those moments you never forget. I thought then, *yeah, this job's all right*."

"From the flight deck? That's incredible! Wow, what a sight." Josh shook his head. He really needed to see more of the world.

"But this place…this is the best place I've ever been. I'll always come back to St Seb's."

"I would too, if I could!" Josh turned his head to look out of the window. Somewhere in the darkness was that clear, unsullied sea. He was quiet for a moment, before saying, "You know how people say they went traveling and found themselves?"

"I've heard it once or twice," Guy murmured between the kisses he was dotting along Josh's shoulder.

"I always thought that was a load of old hogwash. I mean, how can you find *yourself*? You know very well where you are! Most of the time. A couple of times at uni I got plastered and didn't know where I was, but only for a short while!" Josh chuckled, then he went on. "But the strange thing is, since coming to St Seb's, I sort of…know what that means now. I always thought I was sensible and didn't take risks, and I thought I was happy like that. But…but I don't think I really was. I'm happy now, though—*very* happy. And I'm not being particularly sensible at all."

"When I asked you out to dinner back in London, I didn't expect any of this." Guy's voice was soft, as soft as the kiss he placed on Josh's cheek. "I'm very happy too, darling, how could I be anything but?"

"We've done a bit more than have dinner!" Josh put his glass aside and ran his hand over Guy's thigh. "Although that big plate of food I had at the beach bar counts, doesn't it?"

"Sort of. I'm still going to treat you to somewhere special when we get home though." *Home*. It sounded perfect in that smooth voice. "If you fancy it, of course!"

"Of course!" Josh closed his eyes and pictured Guy in his cravat again, piloting his sports car with assurance and ease. "I don't want a holiday fling, Guy. You're too special for that."

Guy kissed Josh's cheek again and whispered, "You're wonderful, Josh, every sensible, floppy-fringed bit of you."

Josh drew his hand back through his hair. "Maybe the fringe isn't sensible! Maybe you spotted the un-sensible me trying to get out!"

"Maybe," Guy murmured, stroking his fingertips over Josh's thigh. He paused when he reached his reawakened erection and drew his finger along the length, then observed, "You're very passionate too, though. That must be the poet in you."

Josh sighed with pleasure. He reached one arm up behind his head, resting it against Guy's neck. "I'm glad you think so. I'll have to have a go at writing a poem. For you."

Guy chuckled gently, tightening his fingers around his lover's erection. When he began to stroke, his pace was lazy, and all the time his lips were on Josh's skin, roaming his jaw and neck, teasing at his earlobe.

"Sorry for *that* coming up again...it's just, you're so..." *I'm going to struggle with that poem.* Josh thrust against Guy's hand, trying not to laugh as the water splashed back and forth in the bath like waves. "I love the way you touch me."

"You're lovely to touch," Guy replied. He slipped his other arm around Josh's waist and slid his hand over his chest until he could gently caress his nipple. "Every bit of you."

Josh half-closed his eyes, reveling in the strength of Guy's body that surrounded him. Those wonderful arms around him, and the broad chest behind him, and those elegant, firm legs holding him between. "I've always liked an older sort of man. People think it's silly, but you're so attractive… I just melt."

"That's probably a pilot thing," was Guy's playful response. "So you've got a fancy for a mature kind of fellow? You get better every minute, darling!"

"All part of being sensible, you see!" Josh paused as a deep moan went through him. "Mature men know what they're doing. And you *definitely* — oh, Guy — you definitely do."

Every sensation seemed so alive, from the exotic fragrance of the bath to the heat of the water and the lingering taste of champagne, but more than that was his lover's touch. Guy was the experienced man he had always wanted and now, prudent or not, he was falling in love. And falling in love with Captain Collingwood felt marvelous.

Josh gave himself over to Guy and to his climax, with hope in his heart that Guy was falling in love with him too.

Josh didn't have a thought of anything beyond Guy, beyond his kisses and their whispered words of passion and the wonderful moment when their bodies were united. As a breeze from the ocean stirred the curtains, their caresses were softer still and time ebbed away around them, here in paradise.

Chapter Eight

Josh woke up in Guy's arms again. He couldn't think of anywhere nicer to wake up and turned his head to kiss Guy's cheek.

"Morning…" he whispered.

Guy's eyelids flickered for a moment before he opened his eyes, his gaze as filled with merriment as ever.

"Good morning, best man." He snuggled Josh closer. "Was it a nice sleep?"

"A very nice sleep." Josh nuzzled against him as a high-pitched wind whistled through the palm trees outside and the waves thudded along the beach. "It's so cozy in here, with all that wind outside!"

"Fingers crossed this is as bad as it gets." Guy kissed Josh's hair, letting his lips linger. "I never asked how it went yesterday, darling, we were too busy falling for each other! Were rehearsals okay?"

"Depends what you mean by *okay*," Josh said. "If it means the bride nearly had a meltdown because she'd left her *something blue* at Heathrow, and one of the bridesmaids may or may not be intriguing with a waiter who just so happens to be Pierre's nephew, then yeah, it went okay. I know I shouldn't say this, but my god, Rey's mum is terrifying. Then the bride's mum was being terrifying too, and if it hadn't been for Rey's dad and Pierre being really laid-back, then there probably would be no wedding at all!"

"Vadim's been cozying up to a bridesmaid?" Guy gave a hearty chuckle at the revelation. "Well, she could do a whole lot worse than that! Why do mums get so worked up when it comes to weddings? It's supposed to be a day to celebrate love, but we see them out on the beach all the time and they look more stressed than happy until the show actually gets on the road. *Then* they relax, so hopefully you've seen the worst of it and today will be all romance and roses."

"Maybe that's why champagne was invented — to make the mums chill!" Josh rested his head on Guy's chest. "Poor Rey was *not* enjoying himself. I think he just wanted a simple wedding on the beach, and various family members have conspired to turn it into the wedding of the century, no slip-ups allowed. It would seriously do my nut if it happened to me."

"Been there, done that, got the battle scars to prove it," Guy told him with a smile. "The casual weddings we get out here once in a blue moon always seem much nicer. Just one big party with marriage vows. Everyone's relaxed, nobody's dressed in a boned meringue... But each to their own, I suppose. If boned meringues are your thing, then good luck to you!"

"I'm not sure one'd suit me!" Josh grinned. "Unless I develop a taste for drag. And, well, I'd need a fiancé first, of course." Realizing his cheeks were burning with embarrassment, Josh tipped his head to one side. That was part of his red face hidden from Guy, at least.

"Well, who knows what the future might bring," Guy breathed, stroking his fingers over Josh's shoulder. "Everyone's got wedding fever at the moment. Teri and Noah got engaged yesterday, so I'm losing my partner in crime *and* my best purser in one fell swoop! I can't imagine they'll trade St Seb's for England once they're hitched."

"It's nice here even if the weather's a bit ropey!" Josh gazed out of the window at the bending palm trees. "I really don't want to get out of this bed, but I suppose my tuxedo calls. Don't want to find Rey banging on my door!"

"What time do they need you?" He heard Guy reach out for his watch on the bedside table. "I assume you've got to be there to straighten ties and pose for thousands of photos?"

"Oh, yes. I was sent a timetable two months ago." Josh rolled his eyes. "I've got to be in my tux and on the beach for eleven. Dare I ask what time it is now? Please don't say 10:45!"

"It's just gone eleven."

The bed, the whole room, the whole house, the entire island, seemed to lurch. Josh froze, staring in wide-eyed panic at Guy. "Oh God, no, Rey's mum really *will* feed me to the sharks! I've got to go!"

"So that was a really, really bad attempt at a joke! It's just turned nine." Guy caught Josh in his arms and grinned. "Sorry, darling, you've gone drip white!"

Josh puffed out his cheeks. "*You'd* turn white if you'd ever met Rey's mum! She'd feed *you* to the sharks as well! *Phew.* We can cuddle for longer. Don't suppose you've got cinnamon buns for breakfast? Or just lovely firm buns?"

Josh reached beneath the bedsheet, down to Guy's hips, and stroked the side of one very firm bun indeed.

"Luckily for us, I can provide both," Guy told him. "And I've even ironed a shirt and polished my cufflinks ready to be your plus one."

"Do you think we've got half an hour? Maybe?" Josh asked hopefully.

"It's only a short walk back to your place, so we've got at least half an hour." Guy's hands caressed Josh's back, smooth against his skin. "Then I'll see you safely home, darling."

"Can we have buns in bed?" Josh raised an insinuating eyebrow. He suspected that Guy wouldn't mind at all if they got crumbs in the bed.

"Are you allowed a naughty Buck's Fizz or are you on the fruit juice and tea this morning?"

"Sod being sensible—I'd *love* a Buck's Fizz." And if they'd had more time, there was something else Josh would have loved too.

"That's the right answer!" Guy kissed his hair. "Keep the bed warm, First Officer, I'll be back with buns before you have time to miss me!"

Josh pushed himself up against the pillows, keeping one eye on the weather outside. It was blowy, that was for sure, but maybe it'd wear itself out and leave them with a sunny day instead.

Hopefully.

He watched Guy as he left the bed and stretched, giving Josh ample time to admire those *other* buns, and Josh had a feeling that was why Guy had done it. His wonderful peacocking pilot was never shy, after all.

Then he padded across the room to retrieve his robe from a chair and pulled it on.

"Just in case Teri's in residence," Guy explained as he knotted the belt. "Don't want to give her a fright over her cornflakes!"

"I'd say she'd be getting a treat!"

Guy laughed and replied, "She might not agree!" At the door he paused, turning back to Josh. For a moment he was silent then he said, "You know, I don't think I've ever been happier than I am right now. Thank you, darling, for the necklace and the kisses and for just being *Josh*. Sensible or otherwise."

Josh blinked at him. He couldn't remember anyone saying that to him before. "Thanks for being my captain," he replied.

My captain.

He let the thought warm him while Guy was gathering their breakfast, losing himself in daydreams of the two of them at the wedding, Josh in his morning suit and Guy — he hoped — in uniform. Even the week he would have to endure in England while his captain was still enjoying the Caribbean sun didn't seem too arduous because at the end of it, there'd be a reunion to look forward to and he'd be in Guy's arms all over again. If this was what falling in love felt like, no wonder people got so excited about it.

Outside the waves seemed to be crashing against the headland harder than ever, but Josh hoped that on the beach things might somehow be calmer. Perhaps there was more shelter from the mainland there, he reasoned. Perhaps the wedding on the white sands of St Sebastian might still be a possibility, and if not, the hotel was luxurious enough to keep any bride happy.

Even Stella.

"I think we're alone," Guy announced as he slipped through the door, carrying a tray piled high with fresh fruit and cinnamon buns, as well as a sparkling and very generous jug of Buck's Fizz. "Teri must still be celebrating her engagement!"

"If only every day started like this!" Josh drew back the sheet and plumped Guy's pillows up for him. "That said, if they did, I'd never get out of bed."

"I'm going to miss her, you know," Guy admitted as he set the tray down and unfastened his robe. "I know I've not exactly shone as a dad but Teri was always a bit of a second chance. Her pa and I flew together for years and she was only a girl when we lost him. I hope she thinks I did all right after her pa passed on. Filled in the gap before her mum got hitched again and all that..."

Josh held his hand out to Guy, drawing him into the bed. "She's obviously very fond of you. Are you going to help out with her wedding, by the way?"

"Well, it's funny you should ask that." He smiled, kissing Josh's cheek. "Because you might not be the *only* senior wedding chap in Gosh before too long. She wants me to give her away and her stepdad has apparently said he's more than happy for me to do it. But I think we should *both* do it, me and him. What do you reckon?"

Josh slipped his arm around Guy. "Both would be adorable. Have you suggested it?"

"Not yet, but I'm going to." Guy picked up the tray from the bedside table and put it carefully on his lap. "I do wonder if my boy's married, you know, but...I don't know if I want to know. Because then I *know* he's done it without me and that feels sort of final, doesn't it?" He shook his head and sighed. "Right, that's enough angst for one year! Buns, booze and boyfriend, that's all I need right now!"

"Maybe you'll find him soon. I could help, you know." Josh kissed Guy on the cheek, then helped himself to a cinnamon bun, which had a starburst pattern in icing on top of its spiraled pastry. "Now this looks better than the one at the airport!"

"Made by the fair Una, Teri's mother-in-law-to-be!" Guy poured two glasses of Buck's Fizz and put the jug out of harm's way on the bedside table. "She likes you, in case you're wondering. She thinks it's about time, apparently! I don't know what it is about me, Josh, but I have mums everywhere looking out for my best interests and plying me with cake."

"About time you lounged about in bed with your very own pearl-diver poet merman?" Josh took a glass and raised it in salute. "I think they might be right. I certainly know it's time I drank Buck's Fizz in bed with a hot pilot."

"And wouldn't you just know that I've been searching for a red-hot HR manager!" Guy clinked his glass against Josh's. "Especially one who's a pearl-diving poet merman in his spare time. We're made for each other!"

Josh nestled against Guy and kissed his shoulder. He grinned up at him. "Best breakfast ever?"

"Best since yesterday." He smiled. "I've a feeling that's just life with Josh."

Josh nodded as he bit into his cinnamon bun. Crumbs fell onto the bed, but he left them there, making no attempt to brush them away. There were crumbs on Guy's chest too, he noticed. That broad chest that felt so good to snuggle up to.

"God bless cinnamon buns," Guy sighed. "Bringing lovers together!"

"Would you like me to sort out your naughty crumbs?"

"Oh well, since you're offering…" Guy put the tray aside and ran his hand down Josh's cheek. "I wouldn't say no."

Josh pressed his lips to Guy's then, before they could be distracted by a kiss, he roamed his kisses south, down Guy's neck and onto his chest. Josh tweaked Guy's nipple as he kissed his way over the chest, licking each crumb up with tender effort. Now *this* was the best sort of serving for a cinnamon bun—a broad, firm chest, with a heartbeat against his lips.

And was there ever a finer sound than Guy's soft moans and sighs, or the way the breath caught in his throat as he reached up to tangle his fingers in Josh's hair? He felt Guy's nipple grow harder at his touch and marveled again that this man was his.

And somehow Josh would have to get out of this bed and go to a wedding.

No, I'm not thinking about that.

Because now there was something far more tempting for Josh. He straddled Guy's hips and, although most of the crumbs had gone, he drew shapes on Guy's chest with his tongue.

Guy's back arched and he gave a groan that was pure desire, topped off with an irresistible heat. *My captain…*

"Josh," he gasped, Guy's voice sending a fresh pulse of excitement through Josh. "God, that's good…"

Josh moved farther down Guy's body, circling his tongue in Guy's navel. He took Guy's erection in his hand and pouted toward it before asking, "I don't suppose you'd like me to lick *all* of you? I really should, just to make sure I don't miss any crumbs."

"You better had," Guy replied in a breathless voice. "Just in case…"

"As you say, it's good to be sensible sometimes." Josh winked at Guy, then ran his tongue from the base of Guy's erection slowly up its length to its tip. He didn't look away from him, gazing at Guy's expression of bliss as Josh laved his tongue along his erection again.

He could happily get lost in Guy's blue gaze, as clear and bright as the sparkling sea that surrounded their magical island. All that natural charm, the combination of tenderness and assurance, was beguiling. And sensible Josh, that Josh who had met the glamorous pilot back at the airport, had beguiled Guy in turn. And it was wonderful.

Josh caressed with his tongue, teasing and loving, before he put the tip of Guy's erection into his mouth and slowly took in his whole length. Josh held Guy at the waist, his fingertips slipping around to gently massage Guy's buttocks. Guy's breath caught again and he stroked his fingers over Josh's hair, tangling lightly. Pleasuring Guy was pleasure itself to Josh, as he felt the strength of the man beneath him and sheer manliness of him. What an amazing figure Guy had, and at that moment, Josh was the master of him.

Guy's head tipped back, his lips slightly parted in a sigh of pleasure. His hips lifted just a touch but it was Josh who was leading. Captain Collingwood had surrendered to his lover, and Josh loved it.

Josh went on pleasuring, enjoying every second. As he looked up the length of Guy's body, he pictured the two of them dancing on the beach at the wedding reception, Josh the envy of everyone as he danced in the arms of his captain.

Maybe they'd be dancing at their own wedding reception one day too.

He saw the by-now-familiar tension in Guy's muscles and felt the delicious tightening as his orgasm grew nearer. Every bit of Josh was sensation, focused on his lover's pleasure. Josh intensified his caresses, his own arousal building as Guy's climax approached.

The fingers in Josh's hair tightened then, with a groan of utter ecstasy, Guy's orgasm swept through him. His back arched up from the mattress and his hips thrust against Josh.

Josh lay down beside Guy and held him tight, murmuring softly against his neck. He loved how Guy looked after an orgasm, like a slumbering Greek hero who'd somehow forgotten his clothes. Guy's arm slipped around Josh's waist and held him tight, then he whispered, "Thank you, darling. That was a hell of a wake up."

"When you're up in the sky, will you think of me kissing you just there?" Josh snuggled close to him. "And will you want the plane to go even faster so I can kiss you again?"

"When I'm up in the sky, I'll be wishing I was right here with you." He kissed Josh's hair. "Just like this, cuddled with my man."

Josh was about to kiss Guy again when a sharp bang came from outside. He glanced up and saw a shutter waving back and forth in the wind as if trying to signal distress. But they were nice and cozy and safe in Guy's house. At least, until Josh had to leave.

"Just out of interest," Guy said, trailing his finger down Josh's spine, "what's the best man up to on the wedding night? I assume, since your official duties will all be done, you might be free?"

"Oh, very free!" Josh sighed as he trembled against Guy's touch. "We could always come back to your bed and tidy up the crumbs again, if you'd like?"

"It's a date." He rested his cheek against Josh's hair, breathing softly. "Are you enjoying your holiday, darling?"

"Best holiday ever," Josh replied.

"Much as I don't want you to go, I suppose you ought to be off to get your best man show on the road." Guy sighed. "Shall we grab a shower before we have a wander through the storm? No rain yet, but I don't think this is beach wedding weather."

"We should hop in the shower, yes…" Josh pouted as he peeled back the sheets. "But at least you'll be in the shower too!"

And just like everything else seemed to be with Captain Collingwood, the shower was as sensual as their morning in bed and the night that came before it. The minutes were ticking past, but as Guy went down on his knees beneath the warm water and took Josh between his lips again, he forgot the passing time. Every bit of him was concentrated instead on experiencing *this* moment. He was living at last.

All too soon it was over.

After their shower, Josh picked up his swimming shorts from the windowsill where they'd fallen the evening before. It wasn't a particularly substantial outfit, especially in the powerful wind, which looked as if it was gaining in strength.

"Guy, can I borrow some clothes off you, just so I can get back to my hut?" Josh held up his shorts with a comical grimace.

"Another one of my shirts?" Guy teased then frowned at the shorts. "'Course you can. Help yourself to anything you fancy."

Josh went for a rummage through Guy's wardrobe, emerging with a shirt and cargo shorts. He slipped them on, then tried to slick back his unruly fringe. "How do I look?"

Guy, by now dressed in what Josh knew was his own favorite outfit of shorts and one of his seemingly endless supply of airy shirts, grinned at Josh. "Like the very best of best men."

"Just you wait until you see me in my tux! I'm going to feel ridiculous wearing one on a beach, but still..." Josh bundled up his shorts and buttoned them into a pocket. "I hope I'll look amazing for the slow dance with Captain Collingwood at the reception."

"There's nobody I'd rather slow dance with." Guy held out his hand. "Ready to face some turbulence?"

Josh took Guy's hand. "I'm hanging on to you—I don't want to get blown away!" Although that put a very different image into Josh's mind. "I mean, by the wind..."

"I know *exactly* what you mean!" Guy turned the key and opened one of the glass doors into the howling winds. As if by instinct he wrapped his arm around Josh's shoulders and held him tight to his body, as though that alone would shelter him from the storm that lashed the beach. And Josh had never felt a storm quite like this one.

Josh's fringe whipped him across the forehead and he laughed as he clung onto Guy. "How are we even going to get to the beach?" he shouted over the wind. "Will the sand all blow to Florida?"

"It might take us with it!" Guy shouted in reply. As a strong gust of wind sent them stumbling down from the veranda and onto the sand, Guy's hold on Josh grew tighter still and he steadied them, turning his head as a spray of sand showered down around them. In the few seconds between surges Guy swept Josh clean off his feet into his arms and told him, "Keep your head down, darling, I'm getting you safely back to base."

Josh's heart leaped at such a romantic gesture. He rested his head against Guy's shoulder, never having felt so protected before. Rain fell now, pitting the wetter sand that was too heavy to be stirred by the wind. The gale roared with increasing fury and the waves battered the beach.

He couldn't recall a time when he had felt so utterly cared for as this, so safe despite the raging storm that was building around them. It felt as if nothing could touch Captain Collingwood, even the howling winds of a tropical storm. But Guy was right, this really *wasn't* the sort of weather that made for a good beach wedding.

Maybe it'll calm down in the next hour.

But Josh couldn't convince himself. And how would Guy get safely back to his house?

Once they had rounded the headland and were on the deserted main beach, Josh couldn't see anyone, apart from a couple of hardy souls swimming in the shallows. None of the sunbeds were laid out across the beach, and the shutters were up on Noah's beach bar, the tables and chairs on the veranda stacked and chained. Even without the spotty towel to act as his beacon, Guy was heading for the right hut. They didn't go up onto the small veranda though, but edged round the side toward the front door where, thankfully, there was finally some respite from the battering wind.

"Well, that was an adventure!" Guy set Josh's feet down on the sand and let out a long breath of relief. "Didn't want you to get blown out to sea!"

Josh slipped his arms around Guy's neck and rested the tip of his nose against Guy's chin. "And I don't want *you* blown out to sea either. Do you want to stay here for now? I'm worried about you getting back home safely."

"I'm going to make a run for it before things get worse." But Guy's arms around Josh's waist didn't seem to suggest he was in too much of a hurry to face Mother Nature's wrath just yet. "I'll text as soon as I get back indoors. Don't you worry about me, Josh, this is just a light island breeze!"

"*Please* be careful, darling." Josh looked round as a child's plastic bucket clattered across the hotel's patio at surprising speed. Guy watched it go, then put one hand on Josh's cheek, keeping it there as he kissed him.

"I'll see you soon," he promised tenderly. "And *when* they decide to move the wedding indoors, just let me know where I need to be. You stay safe, darling, all right?"

"I will. I'm not all that sure about staying in this hut during a storm. I might see if I can get moved indoors too!" Josh kissed him, then said, "I really don't want to say goodbye. But seeing you in your uniform at the wedding will be totally worth it."

"You could always move into this little place I know over the headland?" Guy quirked his eyebrow. "Why don't you have a think about it and let me know if it appeals? I hear they do a marvelous breakfast in bed. The best in the islands, according to this poet I know."

Move in?

Was this all going a bit too fast? But it was only for the remainder of his stay—it wasn't as if Guy was inviting him to cohabit permanently. "I'd really, really love to. I'll pack now, and after the wedding I'll only need to grab my suitcase!"

"You should know that I'm an incurable old romantic." Guy smiled, just the hint of a blush on his cheeks. "And if that's too much, too soon, I'd understand. But if it's not too much, too soon, I'd love you to stay at my place before you have to answer the siren song of Basingstoke."

Josh tweaked Guy's pink cheek. "I don't want a waste a moment—of course I want to stay with you. Imagine waking up every morning like we did today? I'd be a right idiot to say no to that!"

Guy beamed, then pressed a soft kiss to Josh's lips. "Stay safe, Mr. Robertson, and I'll see you very soon."

"See you, darling. I'm going to wait here and watch you go round the headland before I go inside." Josh held on to the door handle as another gust roared over the beach. With one more kiss, Guy finally took his arm from around Josh.

He smiled again and said, "I'm off to get into my party frock," then turned away and jogged down onto the beach.

Josh peered around the corner of his hut and watched as that fine figure of a man ran through the storm as easily as if it was a breezy day in Surrey and not the edge of a tropical hurricane.

I love you, Josh mouthed to Guy's retreating back. *Stay safe, darling.*

"Josh?" He heard a woman's voice call his name as Guy disappeared around the headland. "You got a minute?"

Josh turned and saw Stella there in a toweling robe, her face shiny without makeup and her blonde hair in rollers. "Yeah...come on in."

Was this usual for the best man to be visited by the bride on the wedding morning like this? Josh took his key from the pocket of his swimming shorts and let Stella into the hut.

"I...I've met this amazing bloke, Stella... I may not have stayed in my own bed last night!"

"That's really sweet." She smiled — sort of — then her face crumpled and fat tears began to roll down her cheeks as she said, "I really need someone who's not a mum or a bridesmaid to talk to, Josh! I need a gay mate!"

Josh put his arm around Stella and sat her down on the side of his perfectly neat, unslept-in bed. He gave her a hug. "Let's be nice and relaxed. Enjoy the magic of St Seb's!"

She sniffed and nodded, hugging him in return. This was normal pre-wedding nerves, surely? It wasn't a full-on meltdown. It couldn't be.

"Everyone's shouting about the weather and freaking out and I wish we'd just gone to Vegas or something and never come here and Rey's mum is going on and on and on about the island and —" She finally took a breath, then surged ahead again. "We all get on really well usually, but since Rey suggested St Sebastian she's just been permanently angry and really stressed! And he just mentioned his dad last night and Pris went through the roof. I want a nice wedding, Josh, not...*this*!"

"You mean Rey mentioned his biological dad, not Martin?" Josh hugged her, trying to avoid the tiny spines on Stella's rollers. "I was thinking at the rehearsal that Pris was stressed, wanting your wedding to be perfect because her first marriage wasn't. But at the end of the day, I suppose it's only natural at a wedding for Rey to think about his dad. Pris is being a bit of a dick if she can't see that. It's a special day for you and Rey, and everyone else should feel lucky they've been invited, not see it as an opportunity to boss you about."

"I tried to get in touch with his *real* dad, but I couldn't." She rested her head on Josh's shoulder. "I found him on Facebook and I typed out this long message trying to explain but... When it came to it, I daren't send it. And I *know* Rey wishes his dad was here really, but he doesn't want his mum to know. And he doesn't want to admit it to himself either, or Martin, but Martin's amazing, he wouldn't mind and — "

Another sob escaped and she shuddered, her tears damp through Guy's shirt.

"Shhh... Shhh..." Josh patted her shoulder. He was glad Rey had found Stella — that Rey had someone looking out for him. He couldn't imagine how frustrating it must've been for Stella to be that close to speaking to her future father-in-law but having to hold back. "It's okay. Maybe when we get back to England, you can message him then? I'll help if you need a hand. Seems like a best man thing to do. But not today. Poor Rey, it's not fair when kids get caught up like that when their parents split up."

"I bet they've sent a search party out." She lifted her head and managed a teary smile as across the room,

Josh's phone buzzed. *He's safe.* "Will you really help me get this sorted when we get home? Rey and his dad?"

"Yes, I promise I will." Josh kissed the top of her hair. "This new man of mine… He has a son he's lost contact with, and when I was telling him about your wedding, he looked so sad for a moment. Wondering what his own son was up to. So if I can help reunite Rey and *his* dad, I definitely will."

"You're the *best* man. I can't wait to meet your boyfriend, I hope he knows how lucky he is." She wiped her eyes and pecked a kiss to Josh's cheek. "I suppose I'd better go back to the mums and make myself look like a proper bride. Fingers crossed this storm just does one, I can't have the hassle of that going wrong too. Pris'll explode!"

"Imagine—massive earrings and kitten heels strewn for miles! Now, I'd offer you a tissue if I had one to hand, but…" Instead, Josh used the cuff of Guy's shirt to wipe at Stella's tears. "Big hug for the bride, then I'm hopping into my tux!"

"Big hug." Stella smiled, throwing her arms round him. "We all love you, Josh. You're so sensible!"

Josh hugged her back. "You wouldn't think that if you knew what I've been up to lately, but I blame this fab island for that!" *Goodbye, sensible Josh! Hello, romantic Josh.* "You'll meet my man later. You'll swoon, I promise!"

"And when *you* need a bridesmaid," she teased, "I might know just the girl!"

Stella kissed his cheek and rose to her slippered feet. "I'll see you later. You can read your man's message now!"

Josh opened the door for her. The child's bucket was still doing circuits of the patio. "Do you think the wind's quietening down a bit now?"

"Let's just tell ourselves yes and cross our fingers?" She scrubbed his hair and hurried away, her rollered head bowed against the storm.

Josh watched her go, then checked his phone.

Safely home. Time for a cuppa then into my glad rags. Can't wait to see you. Xxxxx

Josh replied, *Safe trip back to the beach later! Slow dance at the wedding reception for Gosh. Packing and tuxedoing now. xxxxxx*

Love was very definitely in the air.

Chapter Nine

The wind had got up again, so strong now that it was turning the waves into mountains of foam. By the time Josh had packed and got into his tux, the wedding flowers that decorated the chairs set out for the wedding had been blown out of shape, their petals scattering over the sand.

Josh was stopped in his tracks by a blast of wind that came out of nowhere and carried with it a lilo and a plastic chair flying three meters above his head. He ducked and struggled on against the fierce blast, his tie whipping his cheek with each gust of wind, sand rasping his cheeks. Ahead, he saw the wedding party clinging for dear life to the lectern set up for the marriage ceremony.

"Rey!" he shouted against the roar of the wind. "We should be indoors, mate!"

"They said at the reception desk that it *should* just clip the island and move on, but it's not feeling very *clipped* to me!" Rey turned to the minister, the man Guy had identified as Una's husband and Noah's father. "What do you reckon? Have you had weddings in worse than this?"

"Sometimes!" The minister's reply was almost snatched from his mouth by the wind. "Could we wait half an hour?"

Josh couldn't imagine Pris waiting for anything. She had run the rehearsal as if drilling troops. She'd even made them synchronize their watches. Martin held up his hand and turned to Pris, who was waiting in the inadequate shelter of the palm trees with the bridal party. Josh couldn't hear what was being said, but eventually Martin shouted, "If you think it'll help!"

Then he saw Guy.

Not naked and drowsily satiated as Josh liked to picture him, nor casually dressed in one of his loose shirts like the last time he had seen him, but resplendent in uniform, his cap tucked beneath his arm as he strolled over the sand toward Josh. Even gale force winds didn't seem to faze his captain.

Josh started to jog toward him over the beach. He waved, but just as he did, he heard a shriek. Josh stopped. Had someone been hit by a flying sun umbrella? But as he turned he saw Pris, her hand over her mouth. She looked suddenly haggard, and Josh couldn't grasp what had caused her to change so abruptly. Surely it wouldn't matter too much if the wedding was delayed a little, or even if it was held indoors?

But his answer soon came as Pris yelled against the wind, in Guy's direction, "What the hell are *you* doing here?"

"I'm going to a wedding," Guy replied, a look of utter bewilderment on his face. "What're you —"

Rey was thundering over the sand though, his voice raised into a furious shout. "I told you, you're out of my life! How dare you show up at my fucking wedding like— How dare you?"

"You're not a part of this family anymore!" Pris wailed. "You deceived me and walked away!"

Josh stared. Words crashed against his skull with the force of the storm-churned waves thudding along the shore.

'I have a son and the divorce was a mess.'

'Martin's my stepdad.'

Rey was Guy's son.

The ground lurched under Josh's feet again and it was only the force of the wind that held him up.

He shivered.

I went to bed with my best friend's dad.

Guy's gaze flickered to Josh, filled with both a warning and such pain that he could almost feel it. He gave a barely perceptible shake of the head, as though telling Josh, *say nothing.*

Is he really going to try and keep me out of this?

"There's been a mistake," was all he said, looking at Rey now. "I'm sorry."

"Yeah, you bloody should be!" Rey bellowed. "You're not welcome. *That's* my dad, not you!" He jabbed his finger toward Martin. "Now get away from my wedding!"

As the words left Rey's mouth, the wind seemed to reach a new ferocity and the flower-covered archway beneath which the happy couple were to be wed lifted off and sailed toward the ocean.

And for some reason, Stella went with it.

She gave a howl of terror as she was dragged across the sand, her veil tangled hopelessly in the thorns of the roses that were entwined around the archway. Her hands clasped desperately at her hair as she stumbled back into the ferocious waves and the veil finally came free, a moment before the arch dropped down and landed with a sickening thud against Stella's forehead.

Nothing felt real anymore. Not the storm, not the pain burning in Josh's heart.

He didn't think about anything other than the life-saving lessons he'd taken at school. Josh threw off his hired jacket as he ran down the beach, not giving a stuff about the deposit, and toed off his shoes. The waves were so strong, and he couldn't see Stella for all the white foam kicked up by the wind. Everywhere he looked he seemed to see her wedding gown.

The floral arch rose and fell on the waves, the flowers adorning it torn away and washing up on the shore. Then Josh saw it, a flash of golden hair among the waves farther out. He strode through the water, then dived through a rising wave. Within a few strokes, his hands became entangled in what had to be the train of Stella's dress. Forcing his eyes open in the salt water, Josh saw a human shape, and he slipped his arms around Stella's waist, then kicked hard and pulled them both up to the surface.

As he swam back to shore on his back, with Stella against his chest, he pressed his fingers to her neck.

There's a pulse, thank God.

"She's okay!" Josh yelled. He was aware of figures gathering along the shore, but the waves were crashing over both him and Stella and his eyes were stinging from the salt. Once he was in the shallows, Josh could stand, and he staggered toward the beach. Stella moaned as he carried her, seawater running from her coral-painted lips.

Guy, immaculate, well-groomed, dashing Guy, ran through the surf with Rey a few feet behind, both men nearly knocked off their feet by the winds. They reached Josh as one and as Rey reached for Stella, Guy put his hand to Josh's face, gazing at him with a look in his eyes that Josh had never seen in his life.

"I thought I'd lost you," Guy admitted, and Rey looked first at him, then at Josh. Then he looked at Guy again and realization dawned on the young man's face.

"Oh, you rotten bastard," Rey murmured, a moment before he punched his father in the jaw.

Stella had found strength from somewhere and groaned. "Rey! For God's sake!"

She forced her way out of Josh's arms and he allowed himself a moment to sag before he attempted his sodden walk up the beach.

All at once, the sky turned upside down and he saw nothing but a crystal wall of sea.

Chapter Ten

Josh awoke in Guy's bed. For a moment, he wondered if the disastrous wedding had only been an anxiety dream, but when he realized how much his head was throbbing, and that his skin was crusted with salt, Josh knew the fiasco had been all too real.

He rolled over and tried to peer through the gauze curtains around the bed.

"Guy, are you there?"

"I'm here." Josh, it seemed, had rolled the wrong way. With some effort he managed to turn, and there was Guy, sitting on the edge of the bed. He was far from immaculate now, his jaw showing a purple bruise, the uniform he still wore drenched and stained with salt water. He dipped his head and kissed Josh's hair. "Bloody hell, darling…"

Josh reached for Guy's hand. "Is Stella all right?"

"She's fine," he promised, kissing Josh's hand. "Because of you."

"I did life-saving lessons at school. Just in case." Josh tried to smile. "I've never had to do that before. I didn't think twice. Where — where are the others? Rey's going to kill me…"

"They went back to the hotel." Outside came an almighty roar as the storm battered the walls that sheltered them. "I didn't know— Rey? He's Freddie. Where does Rey come from?"

"Sorry…it's just a stupid uni nickname," Josh explained. "Freddie Reynolds. I used to call him Debbie, as in Debbie Reynolds, but that was a bit too camp so I ended up calling him Rey. He used to get called Reymundo, Rey-Rey The Reymeister…"

How bloody awkward. I went to bed with my best friend's dad.

"I brought him here after we got divorced," Guy admitted. "Before it all went wrong. I had no idea, Josh, honestly."

"You couldn't have done. And nor did I. I didn't know until yesterday afternoon that Martin wasn't actually his dad. I mean, it's not obvious you and Rey are father and son. You don't look alike at all." Josh wondered if he was headed into dangerous territory by admitting that, but it was true.

"He's the image of my mum," Guy told him. "Martin's been a great dad to him. He did everything he could to keep Freddie and me in touch, but — it was a mess, Josh. I made a mess of it."

Josh squeezed Guy's hand. Looking up at Guy, he could now see the odd echo of Rey's features in Guy's. But he would never have spotted the similarities unless he'd been told the two men were family.

"I can see now why Pris was being such a grump. When they turned up on the island yesterday, she threatened to throw me to the sharks!" Josh widened his eyes in mock surprise. "Bet you've heard worse from her!"

"Once or twice," he admitted, with the ghost of a smile. A gentle knock sounded at the door and Guy asked, "Should I tell them to bugger off?"

"No, it's okay." Josh blinked at Guy. "What are we going to do, you and me? Are you sure you still want to be my boyfriend?"

"I thought—" Guy pinched the bridge of his nose. "All I saw was you swallowed up by the sea. I thought you'd— Of course I still want to be with you, more than anything."

The knock sounded again and Teri called gently, "Cap?"

Josh swallowed down the rising fear in his throat. *We can do it, it'll be all right. It might be awkward at first, but it'll be fine.* But how could it be, when Rey and his father were estranged?

"It's okay, Teri can come in," Josh said. "There's another wedding to arrange!"

Guy crossed to the door and exchanged a few hushed words with Teri. Then he turned back and asked, "Darling, can you spare me for a couple of minutes? Teri's going to sit with you, I won't be long."

Josh tried to push himself up against the pillows. "Yeah...I s'pose. Are you okay, Guy?"

"I will be when I'm back with you." He smiled, slipping through the door. A moment later Teri stepped into the room, looking rather like a woman who'd just battled a tropical storm. Her hair was wild and her face flushed, a far cry from the woman he had met on the plane.

"It's pretty fierce out there!" she announced, settling onto the edge of the bed. "Hey, you."

"Hi!" Josh gave her a wave. "Hope you get better weather for *your* wedding!"

"So, get this" — she stuck her bare feet beneath the sheet — "the storm is *missing* Sebs, this is just the edge of it! They're after bringing some of the hotel guests here, because Guy's place is pretty sheltered by the headland."

Guy's place?

He owns *it?*

"Guy's...?" Josh stared at Teri. "How big is this place?"

"It's not massive, only four bedrooms. I mean, they're massive bedrooms, but—" Teri smiled. "It'll be pretty full in here by tonight, but I don't think anybody'll be getting much sleep. The cap'll just break out the booze and light up the firepit and we'll have a storm party. All the islanders'll come over, they don't even have to ask."

"A storm party?" Josh rubbed his head. "Sounds fun. But it's amazing the storm is missing the island — a chair flew over my head! How strong must it be where it's hit?"

"We've all been lucky. It's sweeping out to sea." She combed her fingers through her tangle of curls. "So...this whole thing with Guy's a bit of a state, isn't it?"

"Yeah..." Josh didn't know where to look. The crumpled bed linen only reminded him of waking up here with Guy that very morning, their limbs entwined. "I didn't know, honestly, I had no idea that Rey — Freddie — Guy... Oh, God, it's so bloody embarrassing, Teri! He's my best friend's dad, and if you only knew what we got up to in this bed...!"

"My dad was a pilot too. He and Guy flew together all the time." Teri hugged her arms across her chest as the wind howled again. "He died of a heart attack when I was eleven and Guy was there for me and Mum every single day. He's been like a second dad to me and when Mum really needed a best friend, he was right there for us. When she married my stepdad, Guy gave her away. He's even teaching me to fly!" She smiled, a rueful look in her eyes. "Whatever happens, he's not going to let you down. You've got a really good man. One of the very best, Josh."

Josh sighed. "I just don't know what to do. I can't hurt Rey—he's my best friend, and there's all this *history* that's just so…it's so sad. If he doesn't want anything to do with Guy, then how the heck can me and Guy be a couple?"

"Your mate won't make you choose though?" She frowned. "That'd be horrible!"

"I don't know, Teri." Josh swallowed. His throat was dry. "It's not going to be easy, is it? And I thought everything was going really well."

"He's lovely." Teri smiled. "It's *got* to work out."

As she said that, the door opened again and Guy entered. He paused on the threshold, offering them both a smile. Then he closed the door and took off his jacket, throwing it over a chair.

"It's going to be a houseful tonight," Guy told them, unknotting his tie. "A few guests from the hotel whose rooms are right in the path of the wind and the usual local storm party suspects. So, Teri, your future husband and the in-laws will be riding out the storm in our sitting room!"

"Where's Rey?" Josh asked. "I need to speak to him."

"You don't want to go out in this," Teri said, paying no heed to Guy as he unbuttoned his shirt and stepped behind a rather ornate screen, out of sight. "He'll still be here tomorrow."

"Are they going to have the wedding?" Josh heard the bang of what was probably a loose shutter against the house. "Stella's dress is a write-off. And I don't even have shoes anymore!"

"But you didn't lose the rings," Guy called. "They're safe on the dressing table."

"That's one thing, at least." Tension drained from Josh's shoulders at that thought. "I tied them onto the belt loop of my trousers with a bit of ribbon—I was worried that if they were loose in my pocket, I might drop them in the sand. As it happens, they went for a swim instead!"

Guy emerged from behind the screen, changed into shorts and a bright blue shirt. Josh saw the shell necklace nestling against his tan skin, a promise of romance between them.

"You won't be disturbed," Guy assured him. "This room's ours, I don't care who's staying over. You saved Stella's life, you know."

"Anyone would've. I just happened to be nearest." Josh shifted under the bedsheet, getting comfortable. He realized he was wearing shorts and a T-shirt. Not his own. Guy must've got him changed after—

"Wait, if *I* got Stella out of the sea, who got *me* out?"

Teri's gaze swiveled toward Guy. He ruffled his hand through his silver-flecked hair but said nothing, so it was left to her to tell Josh, "Captain Guy did."

Warmth spread through Josh as he smiled at Guy. "Heroic Captain Collingwood! I must've been out cold..."

Teri rose to her feet and ambled across the room toward the door. When she reached Guy she squeezed his arm, then continued on her way. She said nothing as she left them alone, but it seemed that Guy only had eyes for Josh. As Teri reached the door there was a fierce knock on it from outside and Rey's voice called, "Josh? Can we have a word?"

Josh glanced at Guy, asking him a silent question. *Should I? Is it okay?* But he knew he'd have to speak to Rey sooner or later.

"Yeah, come on, Rey...I'm still alive!"

Teri opened the door and there was Rey, his tuxedo replaced by jeans and a T-shirt. His face was set with anger and he said, "Can we talk privately? As in without dads who have never really bothered about being dads?"

"Fred—" Guy began, then looked to Josh for his cue. "Do you want me to go?"

Rey's anger wasn't a surprise to Josh, but it didn't set him at his ease. Especially as he was lying in Guy's bed at that moment, signaling as if in neon, *Rey, I've had sex with your dad!* Josh reached out for Guy's hand. "I think...I think me and Rey need to have a chat, darling."

Darling? In front of Rey? What am I thinking?

"Jesus," Rey murmured, shaking his head. Teri shot him a fierce look as Guy squeezed Josh's hand, then released it. As he crossed the room and passed his son, he paused as though to speak. Instead Rey turned away, leaving Teri and Guy to slip from the bedroom, closing the door behind them.

Josh pushed himself up in the bed. He spotted a crumb in the folds of the bedsheets and pushed aside the vision of Guy's chest that morning. When he'd woken up in the arms of his best friend's dad.

"So…" Josh swallowed. "I can kind of guess what you want to talk about."

"Oh, you *think*?" Rey asked, his voice dripping with sarcasm. "I just—he's too old for you, for a start. And you can't rely on him, look what he did to Mum! He's all show and cash, Josh, he's a shit."

Josh's heart squeezed to hear Rey speak about Guy like that. *A shit?* Was the man who had carried Josh through a storm really just that, dismissed in one ugly syllable? "One, he's only twenty years older than me. I've been out with a bloke sixteen years older than me before, it's really no big deal. Your dad's hardly ancient, and he's very well preserved. And secondly, who told you *what he did to your mum*? It wouldn't be Pris herself, would it? You don't think she might be *slightly biased*?"

"Well, if you were a woman and you got married and then you found out that your husband wasn't only gay but was sleeping with blokes behind your back, wouldn't you be *slightly biased*?" Rey challenged. "And now here you are on paradise bloody island and guess what, he's now sleeping with *you*! You don't really believe you're the only one? You don't know him like we do!"

Stung by Rey's words, Josh replied, "Know him? *You* haven't spoken to the man for years! And it's not like I've married him. We'll go on dates back in England, we'll…"

Sleeping around behind Pris' back. Would Guy do that to Josh too? But he couldn't believe that of Guy. He was too tender, too sincere. And if that was all pretend, then Guy was a bloody good liar.

"And while you're not out on a date with him, I guarantee you he'll be on a date with someone else." Rey crossed to the window and looked out into the maelstrom. "You're my best mate, Josh, but... I can't tell you who to sleep with, but this is just too fucking much!"

"Yeah, you're quite fucking right, chum, you *can't* tell me who to sleep with!" Josh pressed the heels of his hands against his eyes. He was crying, and he couldn't cry in front of Rey. And he didn't want to be angry with his friend, but he couldn't help it. "You don't want to hear it, but you need to. How I feel about Guy, I've never felt like this before with any other man. I've never been much of a romantic, but Guy's unlocked something in me, and I...I want to be with him. And he wants to be with me!"

"Do you know what, you can have him. You can have your precious Guy and all his cheating and his lies, and when you finally realize what you've saddled yourself with, give me a call, yeah?" Rey stalked toward the door, his voice wavering with sadness and anger. "But I can't call you my best mate as long as you're with him."

Josh let his tears fall. He was almost too upset to speak, but his anger fueled his words. "You're making me choose? No, you're right, you're not my best mate. Sod off! And you can find a new best man too!" Josh grabbed the wedding rings from the bedside table and threw them at Rey. The ribbon streaked through the room, the rings catching the light.

Perhaps it was the raised voices that brought Guy into the room, and he arrived just in time to collide with his son as Rey left. For a moment the two men looked each other in the eye, then the younger went on his way, slamming the door as he went with such force that it seemed as though the storm had somehow found its way inside. Guy said nothing but instead settled beside Josh on the bed and drew him into a wordless embrace as his tears fell.

Josh couldn't bear to say anything, but after a while he said, "Rey's making me choose. And I don't want to."

There was a long pause before Guy asked quietly, "He's your best friend, isn't he?"

He thinks I've already decided.

Josh nodded. "Best mates since our first day at uni."

"What you said last night about falling in love…" Guy kissed Josh's hair and held him just a little tighter. "I didn't answer because I didn't want you to think I was some stupid old romantic, but I'm falling for you, Josh, which I know probably sounds ridiculous after a couple of days. I'd never ask you to choose, but if you have to and it's Rey's friendship that you need, I'd understand. But it'd never change how I feel about you. I'm just sorry this all had to happen."

Josh smoothed Guy's cheek. "I'm falling for you as well. I've never felt like this before, and…and the thought of giving you up, it's horrible. I may as well have been swallowed by the sea, never to return." Josh tried to smile. "See…you're turning me into a romantic."

"It's a pilot thing," he whispered with a hint of graveyard humor. "I honestly didn't see any of *this* coming."

"And I didn't see the wave that knocked me flying, either!" Josh joked. But he was serious as he asked, "Rey's pretty angry, isn't he?"

"With me, not you." Guy stroked Josh's hair. "Don't worry about that."

"He's my best friend," Josh said, his voice lowered as if Rey was lurking outside the room. Guy nodded, silent, his gaze still fixed on his lover. "Or was. But I can't hurt him, Guy. You do understand? And…" Josh closed his eyes. He didn't want to ask this question, but he knew that if he never raised it, it would haunt him. "I don't know if Rey was just saying hurtful things because he was angry, but he said…he said you saw men behind Pris' back, and he said, he said that you'd do the same to me. I don't want to believe him, but if you're not exclusive, will you tell me before I fall in love with you completely?"

"Not exclus—" Guy's voice was disbelieving, and with the disbelief, Josh heard hurt too. "I can't do more than promise you that I've never cheated on anybody in my life. When Pris and I married I already knew I was gay, but apart from the odd kiss — before we were a couple — I'd never acted on it. If I'm honest, I had this stupid idea that getting married would force me to be straight. I should've told Pris before we got hitched, but I really thought it'd just somehow go away on its own and it didn't. I never cheated on her though, Josh. She and I had been split for months before I even dared look at a man, let alone do anything else. I didn't know she thought that… I didn't know Freddie did either."

Josh twined his fingers with Guy's. He wanted to believe him and he had imagined what life had been like for Guy back then, when he'd got married to a woman instead of being loud and proud. He sounded sincere. And nothing Guy had done since they had met suggested he was a man Josh couldn't trust.

"I understand." Josh kissed their joined hands. "Do you think...do you think she believes that because of all those stereotypes, about gay men tarting about? I can't say I've done much tarting about myself, but..."

"I've always rather favored romance over tarting about." His voice was almost a whisper when he asked, "Are we over?"

Josh shook his head. "I don't want us to be over."

Guy's reply was a very tender kiss and he settled down beside Josh, holding him close as the storm raged outside.

Chapter Eleven

Josh felt better for a rest. His head no longer throbbed, and he was looking forward to the storm party. It was going to be more fun than the wedding reception would've been, with its regimented seating and strict playlist for the DJ.

"Am I dressed okay for a storm party?" Josh asked. He looked down at the T-shirt Guy had dressed him in, showing a map of Trinidad and Tobago. "At least this'll come in handy if I'm swept out to sea!"

"You look perfect." Guy smiled and nodded. He glanced toward the door, where the faint sounds of laughter and conversation could be heard. Josh could already smell food cooking and in the dim light, with the storm raging beyond, it seemed almost dreamlike. "Power's gone, so it'll be a party by candlelight. I wonder who we've got from the hotel? I'm assuming it *won't* be the wedding party. They couldn't have bad luck like that twice."

Josh shrugged. "Tomorrow we'll find out that Pris has stolen a pedalo and is now halfway to Cuba. Shall we go and find out who's here? I'm famished!"

"Well, there'll be a feast if Una's out there." Guy took Josh's hand and helped him from the bed. "But if you feel tired or start to feel ill, I need to know. I'm probably going to fuss, but I'll really try not to!"

Josh grinned. "Fuss all you like, I enjoy it!" He managed to climb off the bed and was steady on his feet. "Look, I'm fine! But I'll lay off the booze, I think."

Hand in hand they approached the door. When Guy opened it onto the vast open-plan sitting room, Josh saw that the storm party was in full swing already and everyone seemed to be having a good time, despite the gale that had almost carried Stella out to sea. Lanterns illuminated the walls and in the center Una presided over a huge firepit where laden pans and trays were warming. She was surrounded by revelers who were eagerly awaiting the fruits of her labors, but everyone seemed to know everyone, Josh realized, wondering who could be the refugees from the hotel.

Noah and Teri had set up an impromptu bar, and Josh waved to them. Then he heard a voice he recognized.

"I'm not trying to make it worse, Stella, don't get on my back about it. It's my best mate I'm losing," Rey was saying. "It's just…you weren't there through it all. He broke Mum's heart."

"Yes, *you're* losing him," Stella replied. "I can't believe you came out of that room, your chest all puffed up like a pigeon, saying, *I've given him an ultimatum!* As if it's somehow impressive. I heard Josh talk about his new man and he really, really likes Guy. Please don't take that from him. Not when we're getting married. Even if it's awkward for you because Guy's your dad."

Josh glanced in the direction of the voices and could now see Rey and Stella between Guy's ornaments on the other side of a room divider, their backs to them.

Unseen by the couple, Guy kissed Josh's hair and whispered, "It's going to be all right. I promise."

"I've made a massive mistake," Rey told Stella. "I don't want to lose my best mate. Do you think— Is there any point me telling him I'm sorry? He's going to tell me to jog on, isn't he?"

"Not lovely, sensible Josh." Stella kissed him. "He came all this way to be your best man—he's not going to tell you to jog on if you say sorry. And funnily enough…he promised to help me find your dad. I'd say he did an exceptionally good job!"

"You were looking for Dad?" Josh felt Guy tense at his side then relax when Rey said with a smile in his voice, "You and Josh're up to all sorts, aren't you? And you're only here because he jumped into the sea after you."

"Exactly. So remember that. If it wasn't for Josh, you wouldn't have a fiancée. Anyway, I should admit… I found Guy on Facebook, but didn't contact him. I did look at his photos, though!" Stella giggled.

"Bloody hell," Guy whispered good naturedly. "God knows what's on there."

"His photos?" Rey asked. "Let me guess. Sports cars, sunshine, jumbo jets?"

"Yes, and walking in Richmond Park, and petting a kitten." Stella sighed. "The kitten one was so cute, and I just knew when I saw that, *Rey's dad's adorable*. I couldn't imagine him turning his back on you if you tried to get in touch."

"I rang him a couple of months ago," Rey admitted. "Well, put his number in and then I thought, *what if he doesn't answer?* So I didn't call. And now he definitely won't answer, because I acted like a fucking moron and punched him."

Josh couldn't help but meet Guy's gaze then. *Like father, like son, after all.*

"You don't need a phone to talk to him now." Stella's tone was gently amused. "Please give it a try. If you want to talk to him, it's up to you. Don't let anyone else influence you. And you do know who I mean by that, don't you?"

"She's still raw, all these years later," Rey told her. "Maybe we should all try and be a bit *less* raw now, though? I just...I don't want me and you to get married and one day he's a grandad and he doesn't even know. We need to sort it. *I* need to sort it."

"Exactly. If we had a child and they grew up and were told one day, *Oh, you've got a grandad out there somewhere but Daddy told him to get stuffed* — it wouldn't be fair on the child, would it? Let's go and find Guy and Josh."

"Maybe not Guy just yet," was Rey's reply, his words sending a fresh pang through Josh. "But Josh definitely. I haven't even said thank you for saving you! When that wave caught you, I just about lost it. We are *not* braving that beach again until the sun's out."

"I did say I wasn't going for a swim until *after* the wedding. My hair's ruined!" Stella tugged at a length of her blonde hair, now matted with sea salt.

"And you're alive," Rey replied. "And alive hair looks way better on you than the alternative."

Josh cringed. He glanced at Guy. "Should I say *hi* to them?"

"Yeah, go on." He nodded. "I'll be over with Teri, trying to be invisible."

"I s'pose this means Pris is here too?" Josh couldn't see her, but the room was packed and the lights were low. She could be anywhere.

"That's why I'm keeping my head down." Guy kissed Josh's cheek. "Good luck."

With his hands deep in his pockets while he tried to hide behind his fringe, Josh headed around the room divider. "Erm…hello, almost-bride-and-groom."

Rey's head flicked round but his gaze dropped away from Josh even as Stella hugged him. "Thank you so much for rescuing me. I have no idea what happened, and I was so scared, then you were dragging me out of the sea!"

"Don't mention it," Josh said. He smiled tentatively at Rey. "Erm…you all right, mate? Things have got a bit weird, haven't they?"

"I thought you'd have better taste than that," Rey told him, just a little cool. Then he managed a smile. "Thank God you were there today. I nearly lost this amazing girl."

"It's all right. I just went in…I didn't stop to think! Other than, *I'm the best man and I've got to make sure the wedding goes okay!*" Josh glanced down at his bare feet, then back up at Rey and Stella. "What's going to happen about that? Can they reschedule it?"

"They reckon so, but that's sort of up to the storm." Rey hugged Stella's shoulders.

"Let's hope the storm doesn't last too long!" Josh tried to smile. He took a deep breath. Keeping all the warring parties apart was going to be impossible now that everyone was marooned in Guy's house.

"Okay, look, Rey…you're my best mate, and I'm going to be honest with you. I had no idea Guy was your dad. Why would I? And he and I, I know it's going to be a really weird thing for you to hear, but it feels *right* being with him. I *really* like him. With time, I reckon I could fall in love with him. Whatever happened in the past, Guy regrets it. You have to believe me. He's so sorry, Rey. He really is. But I don't think he's ever had the chance to say so."

"You don't know him. He's a show-off, he's selfish and he thinks chucking handfuls of cash at you makes up for basically never being around." But Guy had been the first to admit that, Josh realized. Of course he *knew*. "He's not sorry. If he was sorry, how come I haven't heard from him in ten years apart from a check and a card for Christmas and birthdays? I didn't want his checks, I just wanted a phone call!"

Stella patted her fiancé's arm and Rey closed his eyes. Then he said, "I just wanted him to knock on the door."

"He's scared, Rey." Josh put his arm around his friend's shoulder. "You've both been apart for so long, there's this huge gap between you—let's be honest, there's a *chasm* between you. He's scared to cross it. He said to me, he wished you'd phone him, and when I said to him, *why don't you call your son?* he told me he's scared you wouldn't want to talk to him."

"Imagine being married to someone though, having a kid with someone, then he just tells you he's gay, packs his bags and goes? Goes off to be a pilot and swan around and—" He swallowed hard. "To be gay. And he left Mum to tell everyone. How could he do that us?"

"Did he ever tell you why he married your mum?" Josh wondered if he should interfere, but he couldn't see Rey listening to Guy. At least Rey trusted Josh. He hoped.

"He didn't need to. I'll tell you why—because he wanted to, because it suited him at the time," Rey said flatly. "And then he got tired of her."

Stella shook her head. "Just listen to Josh, come on."

Josh gave Stella a gentle smile. "He did it to please your grandad. Things have changed, Rey—it's easier to be gay now than it was. I can't imagine how difficult it must've been for Guy, to be the son of a pilot in the RAF, and to go into the RAF too, and…and he's gay, and he wants to please his father, and he can't be who he really is. And so he married Pris. He shouldn't have—in an ideal world he *wouldn't* have. But it didn't turn out *that* badly, did it? *You* were born."

"He brought me here for a holiday after they divorced and we camped on the beach. I had the best time with him, and— I thought he'd be around more when he left the RAF, but he wasn't." He sighed and shook his head. "And one day, when I was about fourteen, I was in town with some mates and we saw him. He wasn't doing anything, just holding hands with a bloke, and my mates ripped it out of me and I thought, *why did he have to do that?* I mean, you know I'm all right with anyone being gay, but he's my *dad*. And if he never properly loved Mum, never wanted to be with her, then he probably never wanted me either, did he?"

Josh blinked back tears. *What a horrible situation.* But he thought back to their first few days at uni when he had managed to let it slip that he was gay—Josh's choice of *It's Raining Men* at the karaoke had been a particularly large clue—and Rey hadn't minded. Had even sounded *interested* in what Josh's life was like. And it made sense now—maybe Rey was trying to understand his father's sexuality through Josh. "He loves you, Rey. You know it's possible for gay men to want to be fathers—even if they're with another bloke! I'm *sure* he wanted you."

"But even if I wanted to patch it up, think what that'd do to Mum." He patted Josh's shoulder. "But I wanted to get married here, because we'd had an amazing time, me and Dad. And then I bloody hit him, because I thought he'd done it on purpose. I know he hadn't, but I wasn't thinking straight... And I don't want to lose my best mate, either. I'm really sorry, Josh, I've been way out of order tonight."

"That's why he's here, Rey. Because of those happy memories with you." Josh wrapped his arms around his friend. "He loves it so much, he built this bloody house! Come on, I don't want to lose my best friend either. I'm sorry I shouted at you and told you to sod off—I didn't mean it."

"I hope you didn't lose those rings, I'd hate to have to set Mum on you." Rey smiled weakly. "She's been there every day that he hasn't. She's a bit showy, a bit blinging, but she's a good mum, Josh."

"I know...I know." Josh let Rey go. "I know you don't want to hurt her. But...even if you're not a Collingwood anymore, you wouldn't be here without Guy."

"Mum and Martin didn't want me to change my name," he admitted quietly. "But I wanted to be Martin's son and I wanted him to know that. That's the last time we talked, Dad and me. He was *so* hurt and I wanted to hurt him. Dad—Martin—he told me, *you shouldn't do this*, but I was eighteen, mate, just a stupid kid."

Josh glanced over his shoulder. Martin was here, somewhere. He smiled. "That's because Martin's a really good guy. I mean...*bloke*!" Josh chuckled. "Sorry.

But that's really something, for him to try to stop you taking his name."

"He's the best," Rey murmured. "So…this is Dad's place? Still throwing money around, then?"

"Come on, Rey…" Stella said. "He's a BA pilot, he can afford more than just a beach hut at Clacton."

Josh tried not to laugh at Stella's remark. "He's invited everyone over from the hotel because it's safer here. Didn't ask for names, just threw the doors open. If that's chucking money around, he's doing it in the best way."

Even Rey had to grudgingly nod in agreement. His eyes widened then as he realized, "When Mum finds out, she's going to make that storm look like a summer breeze!"

Josh grinned. "The sharks won't be going hungry, at least! Speaking of which, d'you want to grab some food? Una from the beach bar is cooking, and I promise you it'll be amazing."

"That's the minister's wife," Rey told Stella. "Fancy something to eat?"

"*Yes!* It smells amazing!" Stella looped her arm through Rey's.

"Come on…" Josh gestured to them to follow, and they headed over to Una, who loaded their plates with food. He glanced toward Guy, who was deep in conversation with Teri and Noah. The bruise didn't look too bad thanks to the lamplight but Guy, Josh thought, looked wonderful. *My boyfriend.*

He wondered if Guy had seen him talking to Rey. Maybe he had…but would he have guessed what they had spoken about?

"If you two want a drink, the bar's over there." Josh pointed with his fork across the room. "Erm…Guy's there, just so you know."

"Maybe later," Rey told him. "That's not no, it's just not yet."

"That's okay," Josh assured him. "Shall I go over and get you two something? What'd you like?"

"Whatever Stella fancies, she's the bride!"

"White wine," Stella decided.

Josh had predicted that. "I'll see if I can grab a bottle."

He squeezed between the guests, a truly international gathering that included a couple from Alaska and a French family, Argentinians and several British groups. He went behind the bar and slipped his arm around Guy's waist.

"White wine for the would-be bride, please."

"Right away, sir!" Teri teased, turning to gather glasses as Guy kissed Josh's hair. "Just so you know, Josh, it looks like all the parents are in a bedroom somewhere with Noah's pop talking about how to rescue the wedding."

"How's Freddie?" Guy asked him. "All right?"

Where to start?

"I think he's just glad that Stella's all in one piece," Josh replied. "And…I think he wants to come over and talk to you. And he's sorry for punching you."

"Let him get wired into that." Teri put the bottle and glasses down in front of Josh. "And let St Seb work its magic."

Josh picked them up. He kissed Guy's cheek, then said, "Just be honest with him, Guy. Tell him the truth. Tell him what you told me. And make sure he knows that you wanted to be a dad."

He turned.

And collided headfirst with Martin.

"Bet you wish you'd said no to best man duties, eh?" Martin smiled, his eyes crinkling behind the lenses of his spectacles. "I've got a wife spitting feathers in there so I've escaped to get her a glass of vino. Now, I'm no pilot and I've never been in the RAF, but you don't live with Pris as long as I have without learning a thing or two, and what I've learned is that she can bear a grudge longer than Al Capone."

"That *is* true," Guy admitted.

"So I might be about to blow the roof off this place, but I propose peace talks." He looked to Josh for his agreement. "A lad should have his parents at his wedding — *all* of them — this has gone on too long, let's get the lot of us in a room and get this thrashed out once and for all."

Josh nodded slowly. Martin was right, but the thought of Pris blowing her stack loomed largely in his mind. "Okay…I've done mediation at work, and I need to say now — if we do this, Martin, and I *do* think it's a good idea, we have to have ground rules. No swearing, no raised voices, everyone doing their best to stay nice and calm. And…people have got to have space to be honest. Even if it's painful."

"No raised voices?" Guy took a deep breath. "That's Pris out then!"

"And that's not going to help," Martin warned. "It's now or never — you might not get another chance, Guy."

Josh rested his head for a moment against Guy's arm. "Martin's right. We've got to do this, Guy."

Guy nodded and said, "Okay. We can use our room." *Ours.*

Chapter Twelve

Pris perched on the edge of a chaise longue by the window. Her hair looked perfect and unruffled and she seemed to be trying to give the impression that she was placid, but something was simmering. Her lips tightened as if she was trying to rein in her scorn. But at least she'd agreed to give it a go. That surely meant something.

Josh had explained the ground rules to everyone, emphasizing that this conversation was to be *solution-focused, not problem-focused*, and he sat down beside Guy and held his hand.

Guy couldn't be farther from his former wife if he tried, sitting as he was on the bed across the room. Martin and Rey, to their credit, seemed to at least be making an effort to be casual, having taken up positions leaning against a large chest of drawers, leaving Stella to sit with her future mother-in-law. It was Martin who took up the baton first, in that same no-nonsense way he brought to every situation.

"So, this was my idea because I'm pig sick of this family being at war," he told them. "And I don't want Fred to look back later and wish this wedding had been different. We're here for the duration, and we're going to get this sorted."

"Yeah, I'm ready to try and get...I don't know...*something* sorted out." Rey nodded, looking to his mother. "I don't know what, but something."

Pris finally blinked, having stared open-eyed for some time, and plucked at the cushion next to her. "Yes...yes, I suppose...I suppose so."

"Great," Josh said, trying to sound encouraging. "We've all had a bit of a surprise today. Well...four, actually, if you include a violent storm and two near-drownings."

Nobody replied, but every eye in the room was on him.

Waiting.

"Erm...erm..." Josh tried to remember all the times he'd had to do this at work, calming the turbulent waters between warring colleagues. But none of the people in the room with him at that moment were wearing business suits. None of them had fallen out because someone hadn't hit their targets or had been misusing the photocopier or had been making private phone calls on work time. Josh opened his mouth to speak, but he didn't have a clue what to say.

"Priscilla and I were best friends," Guy said out of nowhere, filling the storm-lashed silence. "Military brats who grew up together because our dads were always getting posted to the same places. I remember at my tenth birthday party in Germany, our pas decided that we'd get married one day. Do you remember that?"

Pris crossed and uncrossed her legs. Then she nodded. "Yes. Yes, I do remember that. And you let me win musical chairs, I seem to remember."

"Best friends," he reminded her. "I let you win the sack race when we were twelve too, but I never let on. You just thought you were better at hopping than me."

Pris winced, then, to the surprise of everyone, she smiled. A gentle laugh escaped her perfect scarlet lips. "Yes, I remember winning the sack race — thank you for letting me win, Collingwood!"

"I was a gentleman even then." He smiled. "I come from a military family. The sort of family that expresses fatherly affection by handing over a Jag, not by giving your boy a hug. We grew up on airbases with men who were *men*, and Pris knows what I mean by that. If you had a nightmare, you lay in the dark and pretended to be asleep. If you fell and cut your knee, you laughed it off and went back to the match. In that world, boys don't cry and boys definitely don't get to be gay."

"I grew up in Belfast." Martin nodded, smiling a fatherly smile. "Probably not that different!"

"So, I didn't set out to make a fool of you, Pris, or to hurt you. I wanted Dad to be proud and I *did* love you but…I don't think I knew the difference when it came to loving my best friend and being in love. We didn't really *do* love in my family, just promotions and fancy cars." He glanced at Josh and swallowed. "I was a man to look at, but I wasn't grown up at all."

Josh scratched at the scurf of dried salt at the back of his neck. "It's okay," he whispered.

"I thought you loved me," Pris said, her voice wavering. The wind suddenly picked up outside and a crash from somewhere in the garden made everyone flinch. "You were so romantic, and everyone said I was so lucky, because you were the most handsome man on the base. I just couldn't…I just couldn't believe it when you told me one day…that you're gay. It came out of nowhere."

"And then you left," Rey told him. "And Mum was smashed into bits and you…you just got to keep on being *Captain Collingwood of BA*. You didn't see how much it hurt her. Nobody saw that but me."

Pris sniffed and Stella passed her a tissue. "The rumors going around…horrible gossip I heard. And you weren't there to hear it. *I* was. It was dreadful. People saying that for *years* you'd been with this man and that man and the other behind my back!"

At that, Guy started forward a little and said, "I never cheated on you. Never, Pris. I swear to God, I was faithful to you."

"People always stick their oar in," Martin tutted. "Never listen to gossip, love."

Pris blinked at Guy. She was quiet for a moment, as if deciding how sincere he was. Then she nodded. "Thank you for saying that. And thank you…thank you for not cheating on me."

"And I did what my dad'd done to Fred, I know that. I kept my distance and threw cash at him because I didn't know what he'd think of me. What boy wants to know his dad's gay?" Guy passed his hand over his eyes and when he spoke again, there was a crack in his voice. "He's a credit to you, Pris, and Martin as well. You've raised an amazing boy."

"And he's your blood," Martin said. "Take your credit too."

Stella reached for Pris' hand and held it. Pris was welling up, her gaze fixed on her son.

"I'm sorry for punching you and about your name," Rey whispered. "As soon as I'd done it, I wished I hadn't."

"We begged him not to, Martin and I. You can always change it back, love—it's not too late." Pris blinked again and now a tear ran down her face. Another crash sounded from outside as the wind howled through the palm trees.

"If nobody minds—Stella too—I'd like to be a Collingwood-Reynolds again." Rey pinched his thumb and forefinger against his eyes. "Because that's what I am, really."

"Of course I don't mind!" Stella left Pris' side and gave her fiancé a hug.

She appeared to be on the verge of tears too, then Josh realized that he was crying as well. He ran the back of his arm across his eyes and hoped no one had noticed.

Martin patted Rey's shoulder, then took Stella's empty seat beside Pris.

It couldn't have been that easy, surely?

The howling wind seemed to change then, becoming sharper and more piercing. A thud and another crash echoed from outside and now Pris was sobbing, her whole body heaving with remembered grief. "I just wish you'd said sorry. When you left...you didn't say sorry!"

"I didn't get a chance," Guy protested. "You went ballistic, you threw me out! Bloody hell, Pris, of course I'm sorry."

He squeezed Josh's hand then released it and climbed from the bed, approaching her as though she were a coiled rattlesnake.

"I can't begin to tell you and Freddie how sorry I was—I still am. I lost my best friend and my son and every day, every year, I lost another chance to do anything about it." Guy glanced back at Rey. "I'm sorry, Pris. I really, really am."

"Of course I went ballistic! What was I supposed to do?" Pris' voice had climbed higher in pitch. She turned her face away from Guy. "Just one word — *sorry* — that's all! And you never said it. And you've had all these years to say it and you're only saying it now!"

"So I can't win? Is that it?" He raked his hands through his hair. "I didn't say it then and now I do say it, you don't want to know!"

Pris gripped the cushion beside her, her knuckles turning white. "You've had so bloody long to say it, all these years! Why has it taken you so long?"

"But I've said it! And I mean it!" He opened his arms in exasperation. "I'm not on bloody trial, Pris, I don't have to account for my movements!"

"Too busy gallivanting about like an overgrown playboy, *that's* why!"

Josh winced.

"Mum —" Rey began, but Guy cut him off.

"What should I've done? Put on a hair shirt and moved into a monastery? So my marriage to Pris didn't work out, but nothing that produced a man like you could ever truly have failed. You're my son, Freddie, and I love you." Josh saw his friend blink, saw his face crumple as the fury left him. "And, Pris, you've got the best husband you could ever want. I'm sorry for what happened but *I* get to be happy too and if I want to gallivant about, I'll bloody gallivant. It's allowed, you know!"

"This is his house," Rey told his mother, his voice cracking. "He's sheltering all these people and he doesn't know half of them. He's not exactly…I don't know…Hitler."

"That's a vote of confidence." Guy couldn't help but laugh at his son's unfortunate choice of words. "I may be an overgrown playboy, but I'm not Hitler."

Josh started to chuckle as well, and so did Stella. Pris' racking sobs turned into a gasp, then evolved into giggles.

She rose from the sofa, her legs unsteady, and hesitantly patted her ex-husband's arm. "No. No, you're not Hitler." She glanced across the room, then looked up at Guy with something like awe in her expression. "And you're letting complete strangers into your house to get out of the storm?"

"The St Sebbers made me welcome when I wanted to build this house." He closed his hand over Pris' where she touched his arm. "And because I always have to show off, I made it too big. The least I can do is open the doors when people need a place to shelter."

"Well…" Pris swallowed. "You're a very kind man, Guy Collingwood. Not something I thought I'd ever say, but there we are. And I'm sorry, I suppose…for being so rude to you in your own home, when you'd taken us in."

"Let's call it blunt." Guy smiled. "Is this a truce?"

"Not Hitler and Stalin in kitten heels," Martin said with a sly smile, offering Josh a conspiratorial wink. "Peace in our time!"

"Yes, a truce." Pris held out her hand to shake it, then smiled at Guy. "A hug, perhaps, with my old best friend?"

Guy put his arms around her, holding her close as he murmured, "You won the egg and spoon fair and square, in case you were wondering."

Pris chuckled. When she smiled at Guy, a girlish light illuminated her face. With a cheeky arch of her eyebrow, she said, "And by the way, Josh is very cute. You'll make a lot of people jealous having him on your arm."

"Martin's got a certain dignified charm," Guy assured her. "You go exceptionally well together. Do you fancy a glass of something special? I feel like we've earned it."

"Oh yes, I definitely do!" Pris laughed, then she turned to Josh. "And you look after him, Josh! Or you'll have his old best friend to answer to."

"Do I get a hug as well?" Rey asked, his voice very small. Neither of his parents answered—they simply took him into the embrace, the family reunited at last. The room seemed suddenly, wonderfully serene despite the winds battering the building, and Josh blinked, trying to stop himself from crying. When Rey finally extricated himself from his mother's and father's embrace, there were tears coursing down his cheeks. He brushed them away with his hand and smiled a little shyly, leaving Guy to offer his elbow to his former wife.

With Pris on Guy's arm, Martin offered *his* elbow to Josh. "Looks like you're stuck with me, son. Can I escort you to the booze?"

Josh inclined his head. "Lead away, kind sir!"

"By the way," Rey called, "Dads, you're both invited to the wedding—no penguin suits necessary!"

"That's very kind of you," Guy replied. "I'd say it's your turn to take the family Jag, but I don't want you to think I'm being flash…"

"The XK?" Rey's eyes widened and he replied, "It's a tough job, but I'll do it!"

"I don't suppose you've got a hanky I could borrow, Martin?" Josh asked. "I appear to be damp about the eyes."

Of course he does, Josh realized as Martin passed him a neatly folded handkerchief. He was that sort of man. A Belfast builder who'd never set foot in an office but still managed to navigate a potentially disastrous summit without once uttering the words *mediation* or *safe space*. *Plain speaking*, as he'd probably call it.

And a magical island didn't hurt either.

Chapter Thirteen

Josh stirred from the happiest of dreams late that morning to find himself in Guy Collingwood's arms, and there, in the sunlight of the new day, they made love to the sound of birdsong and softly lapping waves. All that remained of the wedding party was a note signed by Teri, pushed subtly beneath their bedroom door.

Wedding at noon, Una's bar. Dress casual and best man, don't forget the rings – we're on it with the dresses! X

Eventually the two men emerged from their cocoon to discover that St Sebastian had somehow, against the odds, survived the onslaught almost intact. Plastic chairs and umbrellas were scattered among upturned sun loungers, but for the few homes and the small hotel on the tiny island, the damage was slight.

It was something close to a miracle.

Wedding at noon, Una's bar.

Now that's *the wedding of the century*, Josh decided as he and Guy strolled along the sand, hand in hand. *And this is paradise.*

Flowers and bunting and fairy lights had appeared from somewhere to decorate the bar. And Josh had cobbled together an outfit from Guy's wardrobe — a diaphanous white shirt and loose, dark blue linen trousers. The flip-flops would've enraged Pris if he'd turned up to the wedding in them yesterday, but now she only pointed and laughed as she saw them approach along the beach. Josh held up the rings, secure on their ribbon, and gave a thumbs up.

There was no sign of Stella yet, but Rey was there beside Martin, looking not quite groom-like in a pair of freshly pressed trousers and a dazzling shirt patterned with pineapples and parrots. At the sight of Guy and Josh he trotted out into the sunlight and stood before them.

"Your bruise's just about gone. I never was much of a hard case," he observed somewhat awkwardly, gesturing to his own jaw. For a moment Josh tensed, recognizing the same awkwardness in Rey and his usually so-laid-back father. Then Rey threw his arms around Guy and embraced him as he laughed. "Please let nobody nearly drown today!"

"It's going to be perfect," Guy whispered, his eyes closed. "Don't you worry."

And it was.

Josh had to borrow another of Martin's hankies as the simple ceremony to unite two lovers took place in a brightly decorated bar by the ocean. This time Guy wasn't an unwelcome addition to the party but welcomed into the heart of it, positioned in pride of place next to Pris by Rey himself.

It couldn't have been more lovely, the makeshift wedding far more sincere and romantic than the polished-to-the-last-detail ceremony would have been. Even Pris and Angie were friends once more, the mothers and bridesmaids smiling together as they watched the happy couple take their vows.

And there on Stella's arm, something blue — the bracelet Rey had bought that first day on the beach. The bride's dress was borrowed, her mother's necklace she wore was old, and her husband was new.

Noah's sister acted as photographer, capturing every moment of Rey and Stella's happy day. Josh dabbed at his eyes with his sleeves once he'd worn out Martin's hankie, but as he turned from the makeshift altar and saw Guy gazing at him, the tears rising in his eyes were out of love for him.

No, they might not have known each other very long at all, but the warmth Josh felt whenever he looked at Guy was love. He was sure of it, because he was smiling like a fool and he didn't care. He stayed at Guy's side for the rest of the day, never wanting to let go of his hand.

"I love you," he whispered to Guy.

Guy said nothing for a few seconds, an expression of disbelieving wonder on his handsome face. Then he pressed his lips to Josh's ear and whispered, "I love you too, you glorious thing."

And soon England would call them back, but Josh decided to push his usual common sense aside for now. Perhaps Guy was right. Perhaps St Seb's *was* a state of mind.

* * * *

After the wedding, Josh went to his hotel room and packed. He didn't need his little room on stilts anymore as he would stay in Guy's house for the rest of his holiday. As the party at the beach bar quietened down and the wedding guests headed off to bed, Josh and Guy, arm-in-arm, trundled Josh's suitcase home. To Guy's home — *their* home — for the next few days.

"I was thinking about New Year," Guy mused softly as they strolled. "Would it look too flashy to invite everyone over here for my usual party? *Am* I an overgrown playboy? I don't feel like one. I just feel like…life's for living. Just because I'm forty-nine, I don't have to stop being me."

"An overgrown playboy sounds fun to me!" Josh said. "You're right, life *is* for living. If you want to invite everyone over here, then why not? And if someone thinks that'd be flashy, well…let them. They can stay at home with a stack of stale mince pies and the last of the eggnog."

"If they really want to, they can pay for a flight and I'll magically upgrade them." He grinned, then kissed Josh's hair. "I think you and me are going to have a wonderful time, Josh, with loads of cinnamon buns."

They wandered through a grove of palm trees, strung with lights. Crickets rattled in the undergrowth and the waves, chastened now after the storm, susurrated along the beach.

"I'm sure we'll have a great time. It'll be fab to come back again so soon." Josh frowned. "England's going to seem so dreary after being here."

"No, it won't—it's what you make it!" *How wonderfully Guy that way of thinking is.* "And we'll make it wonderful."

"I hope it'll work when we go back to England. *Us*, I mean. Because I do love you, Guy. I don't know how, but I do." Josh smiled at him. "And I'd hate to lose it because we have a misunderstanding at the checkout in the supermarket. It doesn't seem very St Seb's."

"Do I really seem like the sort of chap who'd throw over the finest man he's ever met because of an argument over veg?" Guy touched his forehead to Josh's. "Stop analyzing what *might* happen and just enjoy finding out. There's such a thing as a happy ending."

"I hope so — I really do." Josh kissed Guy's cheek, and they continued on to his house. He was prudent, that was all — he always had been. Josh, the high achiever, the diplomat, the man who didn't fall in love after two days.

And now, somehow, he had.

And it just all seemed far too perfect.

"I have to tell you something though." Guy lifted Josh's case up onto the chaise longue where Pris had sat last night. He turned to look at Josh, a mischievous smile lighting up his face. "I didn't have a clue how to be solution focused versus problem focused. I just knew that I had to tell my son that I loved him."

"That seemed to work, though!" Josh kicked off his borrowed flip-flops and stretched out on Guy's bed. "I'm so sorry your family went through all that in the past. I had no idea...but you know, Rey was always interested in me being gay. I knew he was straight, but I wonder now if he was trying to understand how it worked. So he could understand you better? I'm glad you're all talking now, though."

"I feel as though we're going to be all right, Fred and me." Guy sat on the edge of the bed beside him. "You're very wise, darling, I hope a little bit of it rubs off on me!"

"I'm not wise!" Josh insisted. "My mum's a maths teacher—I've grown up believing that everything has its place, everything has its own logic. See, even St Seb's does!"

"Maybe it's because I have to be very disciplined when I'm flying. Turns out piloting a jet's a rather responsible job, you know!" He saw the mischievous smile return, then Guy snuggled down beside him. "So I like to be anything but when my feet are on the ground. So apply your logic to *us*. Are we part of a grand design too?"

"I think so." Josh caressed Guy's arm with a delicate touch. "You've made me throw up my hands and say *what the hell*. Before, I would've told myself that I couldn't possibly love you so soon, that it doesn't make any sense. But it *does* make sense. I can't imagine being without you, Guy."

"You'll be sick of the sight of me eventually." Guy winked. "Because whenever I'm not flying, I'm going to be safely in your bed."

"I'll be waiting to welcome you home!" Josh slipped his hand under the hem of Guy's loose shirt and circled his palm against Guy's warm skin. "So how does it work, this piloting lark? How long are you away for?"

"Usually a few days at a time—it depends how far I'm flying." Guy kissed Josh's hair. "I'm at home for a couple of weeks every month, but I can give you my schedule. I'm not away all the time, darling, don't worry!"

"Two weeks a month? That's not bad!" Josh unfastened the top button on Guy's shorts. "I can wing it a bit so I can work at home sometimes. Then we can have more time together when you're not thousands of miles away. I *will* miss you while you're off flying, but..." Josh slid his hand inside Guy's shorts. "There...I'll give you something *very* nice to come home to."

"I can see you're going to be *very* bad for early starts," Guy concluded, roaming his lips over Josh's throat. Then he wrapped his arms around Josh, silencing them both with kisses.

Chapter Fourteen

Josh wheeled his suitcase into the lounge and left it by the door, ready to go. He looked out at the bright dawn sky and wished he didn't have to leave. But England beckoned.

"A week without my Guy." Josh sighed, and gazed at his Guy, who was at that moment on the sofa. *First-class lounge, indeed.*

"A week without my Josh," Guy replied with a pout. "And a week today, *Gosh* will be together again and you and I will be in bed!"

Josh crossed the room and knelt on the floor behind the sofa, his arm around Guy. Against his neck, Josh whispered, "I can't wait a week. I want you now."

Guy reached back to caress Josh's face and said in a low voice, "I want you too."

That voice.

It sent an arrow of desire straight to Josh's groin. He kissed Guy's nape, ruffling his hair.

"There's time before we have to leave, isn't there?"

"If you miss your flight, I'll fly you home myself," Guy promised. *If only.*

Josh clambered over the back of the sofa, something sensible Josh wouldn't have been impressed by at all.

"Do you feel *very* saucy this morning?" Josh drew his fingertip down the front of Guy's pristine shirt, hopping over the buttons as he headed down Guy's chest.

"This is your captain speaking," Guy teased, brushing his lips against Josh's earlobe. "And I feel wildly saucy."

"Good. Because so do I."

Josh stroked the V of chest that showed at Guy's opened-necked shirt, then popped open the next button on Guy's shirt and caressed more of that tempting chest. "Whoops, you're so sexy, your shirt is just falling off!"

"It's a pilot thing." He slipped his arms around Josh's waist and drew him closer. "This shirt'll probably be gone before you know it."

The last three buttons seemed to open all by themselves, and Josh parted the fabric so that he could smooth Guy's chest and caress his stomach. "So. Very. Firm," Josh purred.

Guy lifted Josh into his lap for a lingering kiss and whispered, "I love every sensible, romantic bit of you. And I promise you won't have time to miss me."

Josh nibbled Guy's ear as he tweaked his nipple, then breathed, "I just keep thinking how amazing it'll be when we see each other again. I might go wild and run through Heathrow naked just to save time! Then you can have me over the counter in the cafe."

Guy's answering laugh was caught in a low moan. Then he pressed his lips to Josh's and kissed him, his hands nimbly unfastening Josh's shirt at the same time. Josh moaned into their kiss, pressing his hips against Guy as if showing him something Guy would already have noticed — that Josh was erect.

It never takes long.

But such was life with his very own dashing pilot.

The same dashing pilot slid his hands down Josh's exposed chest and wrapped his arms around his waist again, holding him tight. Josh felt Guy's erection pressing against him in turn, the promise of it sending a fresh heat through his blood. Josh began to open Guy's shorts, carefully tugging down the zip to reveal Guy's boxers underneath. Josh caressed down Guy's flat stomach and under the waistband of the boxers, finally taking Guy's erection in his hand with an assured grip.

"Captain Collingwood, I've found something in your shorts. You'll have to go through the red channel when we land... You really should declare this."

"I told you." He unfastened Josh's shorts, his movements leisurely. "It's a pilot thing. We're just made this way."

"You're cleared for take-off, darling." Josh began to stroke him, back and forth, enjoying being stripped by his boyfriend. Guy laughed, nuzzling Josh's throat as he eased his shirt down his arms and threw it aside. Then he teased his fingers lower, taking Josh's erection in his hand and giving it a very leisurely caress.

Josh rocked his hips, a cheeky smile on his face as he went on stroking Guy. He gazed up at him happily, his nearly naked and very debauched boyfriend on the sofa beneath him. Guy blinked up at Josh, his gaze filled with desire when he whispered, "Let's go wild, darling."

"But not *too* wild." Josh drew a condom and a tube from his pocket. "Wild but sensible," he said, and tore the packet open with his teeth.

"Wild but sensible," Guy agreed with a comically stoic nod. "That's my Josh!"

Josh kissed Guy as he prepared him, then he kicked off his shorts, his tan body revealed to Guy. He appeared to be still wearing a pair of shorts.

"In case I forgot to say it today, you're gorgeous," Guy told him, taking his face in his hands. "And I know I've said this too many times, but I love you."

Josh combed his fingers through Guy's hair. "I love you, too, and yes, you have told me I'm gorgeous, but you can say it all you like because it sounds wonderful in your voice."

"I love this thing you have for my voice." Guy kissed him again and whispered in a smooth purr, "You're gorgeous."

"Say it again," Josh pleaded. "Say, *I'm Captain Collingwood, and you're gorgeous.*"

"To my favorite first-class passenger, welcome aboard." Guy kissed Josh's neck. "I'm Captain Collingwood and, Josh, you're gorgeous."

A delighted shiver ran through Josh and he attended to Guy's erection with renewed vigor. "That just makes me *melt.*"

"I'm Captain Collingwood," Guy whispered, "And I want you, Josh Robertson."

"Then have me." Josh shifted so that he was straddling Guy's lap, still stroking him. "I'm all yours. However, wherever, whenever you want me."

Guy closed his hands over Josh's hips and eased him a little higher, teasing the tip of his erection against

Josh's buttocks. Then, as slowly as the kisses he was pressing to his lover's throat, he eased him down.

No matter how often they made love, Josh was never bored of it. He only hungered all the more for Guy. For that wonderful body, and for his assured touch and accomplished movements. Guy was the best lover Josh had ever known, who had been in tune with him from that very first evening they had spent together in the little hut on stilts around the headland.

The island was paradise already, but here, hidden from the world, they made a paradise of their own. It followed them around, followed the kisses and the soft words and the stolen moments. Guy was right. This was a place where magic happened.

Josh moved with him, echoing each thrust, delicious pleasure trembling through his limbs. He placed his palms flat on Guy's chest, feeling the effort in his muscles as he tensed and moved. Was he peacocking a bit? Of course he was. And Josh loved it.

Guy took Josh's erection in his hand, jerking his wrist in time with the rhythm in his hips. He was *definitely* peacocking, Josh knew now, seeing the muscles in his arm tense. His pilot, putting on a show just for him.

Josh was carried away on a tide of passion, and his climax began. He knew Guy would realize, that Guy would hear the tell-tale sighs that Josh always made as bliss began to consume him. And Guy was carried away with him, his kisses growing hungrier, his thrusts deeper as he carried them both over the edge.

"Guy—oh, Guy!" Josh tried to hold on, but with Guy's body joined so deeply to his, he couldn't stop his hips from jolting forward, and he came across Guy's stomach.

"Josh," Guy gasped, letting his head drop to Josh's shoulder as he caught his breath. "Bloody hell, you're perfect..."

Josh ruffled Guy's sweaty hair. "Yes, that was *definitely* saucy."

"Pride of the fleet," Guy told him. "Time for a quick swim before we head out?"

"Very quick." Although Josh was in no hurry to move. "Gimme a couple of minutes first."

"You can stay like that as long as you like," he whispered, kissing Josh's shoulder. Then he slipped his arms around Josh, holding him a in a tender embrace.

Josh closed his eyes, breathing in the scent of Guy's warm skin and his cologne, and feeling the press of their bodies together. *It's only a week, then we'll be together again.*

One long, long week.

Chapter Fifteen

Josh waved hello to the captain of the speedboat as he and Guy headed to the jetty. Then Guy kept walking.

"Guy? The boat's that way."

"One thing about pilots"—Guy swung their joined hands—"we never use boats when there's a seaplane on offer. I thought you might like one more flight with your captain before you head for Blighty."

"Seaplane? I've never been in one before!" Josh almost skipped with glee at the prospect. "And you're flying?"

"It's a last hurrah before Victor sells off his two birds." *The island-hopping service*, Josh realized. *Guy's dream.* "He's off to live with his daughter and her family, and I couldn't let you miss the opportunity before you go."

Josh nodded. If Guy bought Victor's business, then what would become of *Gosh*? But Josh wasn't going to make him abandon his dream for someone he'd only known a week.

"Lead the way, Captain Collingwood!"

Guy was excited as a child on Christmas morning as they strolled. He towed Josh's suitcase along behind him, all the time filling Josh in on the intricacies of the seaplane, which seemed almost as precious to him as his Jaguar. The Jaguar he had promised to Rey, in fact. Yet there was nothing but joy in Guy's chatter, no hint of ruefulness about anything other than Josh's imminent departure.

The modest, tidy airstrip ran parallel to the glittering ocean. It couldn't have been much more different from the vast airport where the two men had met just a week earlier, and Guy's enthusiasm was infectious. He squeezed Josh's hand and pointed toward a small white plane that bobbed on the water.

"There she is!" Guy exclaimed. "Your carriage awaits, sir!"

"This is so exciting!" And so beautiful, the perfect little plane bobbing on the surface of the almost millpond sea.

"And there's Victor!"

Victor was sitting on a low, comfortable-looking deckchair under a faded sun umbrella advertising Martini. Josh wasn't sure how anyone could look more chill than he did, and that was even after the storm that had skirted the island. Victor waved to them and pushed himself slowly up from his chair.

"Guy! She's got a full tank and she's ready to go!"

"Victor, this is Josh, Josh, Victor." Guy left the suitcase and waved to Victor in return. "How could you give all this up? What can retirement offer that this little strip of runway can't?"

Victor chuckled as he came over to them, on slightly creaky legs. He shook Guy's hand, then Josh's. "Retirement—when the day comes when you're happier in a chair on the ground than behind the controls of a plane, that's when you know it's time."

"Have you got a buyer?" Guy asked. "Go on, give me the bad news — who's taking my favorite seaplane?"

Victor shook his head. "No one yet. There was that banker I told you about, who *I* think wasn't interested in the planes at all, but wanted to bulldoze my airstrip and build a golf course. I told him it wasn't for sale when I found that out. But once I've found someone to sell it to, who'll fly the planes, then I'll retire."

Josh grinned at Guy. "*You* wouldn't turn the airstrip into a golf course, would you?"

"Not a bloody chance!" Guy assured them. "It's an island-hopping service, so I'd be hopping islands. St Seb's doesn't need a banker's golf course. Someone'll come along — I'll put the word around with the fliers I know too."

"You still want to fly the big jumbos?" Victor raised an eyebrow at Josh. "I used to, back in the day. Flew for Air France." Victor pointed at Guy and laughed, as if remembering a shared joke between them. "Then one day, I thought, I don't want to spend all that time away from home. I want to be on St Seb's. And so…this is what you see before you."

"I can understand wanting to be here." Guy squeezed Josh's hand. "But the man I love won't be on St Seb's even if I am, and if there's one thing that even *I* put ahead of flying, it's being with Josh. We'll find someone, Victor, don't worry."

Josh blinked at Guy. No one had ever loved Josh enough to give up their dream for him. "But it's your dream. Don't let me stand in the way of it, please don't."

"I'll have her back with you before dinner," Guy told Victor, then turned to Josh. "Ready?"

"Yes." Josh nodded to Victor. "Nice to meet you! I hope you can get back to your deckchair soon!"

"Nice to meet you too. You look after Captain Collingwood, Josh!" Victor smiled, and he threw a bunch of keys toward Guy. "Beautiful day for a flight!"

Guy caught the keys then, as if it was the most natural thing in the world, shot Victor the most glorious salute Josh had ever seen. "Let's go," he announced. "Don't want to keep BA waiting!"

Once Josh was sure they were out of Victor's earshot, he remarked, "You can do that salute again. Preferably when we're alone with a large bed to hand!"

"Even better" — Guy paused at the edge of the quay and opened the door to the plane — "I could do it when we're alone with a large bed and I'm showing you my old uniform from the RAF days. I used to be *Wing Commander* Collingwood, you know."

"Now that I would *definitely* love to see. I'm not even surprised it still fits." Josh tested a foot on one of the plane's floats. "I'm sort of nervous and excited about this — but more excited than nervous!"

"Hop in, you're in very safe hands."

And of that, Josh had no doubt. If he'd stopped to think about *how* this small plane would take off from the surface of the sea Josh might've been rather less excited than he was, but something about Guy's confident manner was as infectious as his enthusiasm, and as they gathered speed and he watched St Seb's begin to rush past, it was safe in the knowledge that he'd be here again in just a few months, ready to see in the new year with the man he loved. The man who'd given up all of this for a chance of happiness as one half of Gosh.

They lifted effortlessly into the air and beneath them, as the propellers whirled, Josh saw the cluster of huts on stilts, the headland and there, shining in the sunlight, Guy's own island palace.

Paradise.

"You're not standing in the way of anything," Guy told Josh once they were airborne. "I want to be with you, not halfway across the world wishing we were together. This is great, but you... You're glorious, remember?"

Josh watched the plane's shadow skip over the clear blue sea below, then he turned to Guy. "No one's ever loved me enough to give up their dream for me."

"Most men never have any dreams come true at all, but you and I have." Guy glanced at Josh and smiled. "That's more precious than anything else, and this island will always be here for us. It doesn't matter that it's just for a few weeks a year, because we'll be here together."

"And we'll have a wonderful time!" Josh saw the mainland advancing up ahead and the plane began to drop in altitude. Josh's island holiday was rapidly nearing its end. "So...Victor's business. It's him and two planes. Or does he have another pilot, and ground crew? Someone in an office selling tickets and keeping an eye on the books?"

"Him and his wife mostly." Guy looked down at the water below them, concentration on his face. "I just don't have the business brain for it and I don't want to get into interviewing and employing people and all that hassle. I just like flying!"

"Okay..." Josh nodded. He didn't speak, as Guy seemed to be listening to someone on his headphones. No, he couldn't...but he *could*...Josh *could* do it. He could sit in an office on the airstrip while Guy flew his planes. And bloody hell, wouldn't a little office on a Caribbean island be nicer than the open-plan barn of a place he currently worked in?

"We're cleared for landing on the beautiful waters of the Caribbean," Guy informed him with a smile. "Then we've got a short walk to the airport and there, though I really don't want to, I have to let you go."

Josh tried to swallow the lump in his throat. But he didn't see England in his mind anymore when he thought of home. Instead, he saw St Seb's. But what about his parents? What about Rey and his other friends?

They landed so smoothly that it felt as if they were still among the clouds and the propellers slowed to a halt as the plane came to rest beside the quay. This might not be first class, but even that wouldn't be so exciting this time, because this time Guy would still be here. And Josh wouldn't.

"Before you know it, I'll be home," Guy told Josh as he took off the headphones. "It'll whizz by. I guarantee it'll seem like no more than a few hours before you see me again."

"I'm going to meet you at Heathrow. Straight off the plane," Josh promised him.

Once Josh was on the quay, he knelt down and touched the water with his fingertips one last time. Then he stood and gave Guy a hug. "Sorry. Just wanted to say goodbye to the sea until I meet it again. Pays to be nice to the sea, doesn't it?"

"That's why I'm never going to take this necklace off," Guy told him as they embraced. "It's a little bit of St Seb's wherever I am, and it's the first gift I ever got from the man I love. And I do have some *very* good memories of the beach now, thanks to you. Not so much the drowning bride as the long, lazy evenings in the surf."

And it was such a short walk to the airport.

Too short.

The grand, glass airport seemed so elaborate to Josh after a week on St Seb's, where no building was higher than three stories. He and Guy hugged at the check-in desk, Josh fearing that security would need to be called to prize his arms from Guy.

"Time to go," Josh said, and ruffled Guy's hair.

"You better had." He laughed. "Teri's on the flight, she's going to look after you, and you've got the best seat in the house. I love you, Josh."

"I love you too." Josh grinned, then pressed his lips to Guy's ear to ask, "Shall I book a hotel for us at Heathrow? Straight off the plane and straight into bed?"

"You leave all that to me," his lover replied. "I've already got plans for our reunion."

"Sounds promising!" Josh grinned. "Will you send me a postcard?"

"I'll probably pass it on the way home," Guy lamented. "You won't have time to miss me. Now go on, before I stop being dashing and start blubbing — and remember, make the best of the bubbly!"

"I'll look out of the window and toast us as we fly overhead." Josh gave him a wink. "Okay…I'll see you soon. And I'll enjoy the hell out of the first-class lounge! Thanks, darling."

"I love you," Guy told him again but as they parted, Josh couldn't look anywhere but at Captain Guy Collingwood, his lover, who kept waving as Josh walked away.

How much better would the first-class lounge have been with Guy beside me?

After loafing in first class, trying not to think about the jumper in his hand luggage which he'd need once they'd landed in England, Josh was at the departure gate. The enormous plane that would be his home for the next nine hours sat on the tarmac, its windows glinting in the sun, glamorous and alluring. So much had changed in the past week that if Josh had collided with his old self in the airport, they wouldn't have recognized each other.

He headed up the tunnel and at the door to the aircraft, met Teri. She was immaculate again, her Yorkshire tones replaced by the well-schooled voice of the head flight attendant who would see them safely over the ocean and home.

"Good morning, sir, and welcome to one of my last long hauls." She grinned, then grabbed Josh's hand and squeezed it. "Me and Noah don't want to wait. I'll be on St Seb's by Christmas! You're *definitely* coming to the wedding. I don't care if the world of corporate HR collapses without you!"

Josh smiled. "I'd love to! And Guy wants to hold a New Year's Eve bash at his house on the island — I'll definitely be there." Josh ignored the growing press of passengers behind him. "But...what'll you do out there? Still be a flight attendant?"

"Una's got the wedding bug and the hotel guests never stopped raving about the food she cooked at the storm party," she told him. "The hotel does loads of weddings and they want Una to be their amazing food guru. She's like Guy though, super talented but rotten at paperwork. So that's where *I* come in. I'm going to be a *wedding concierge*, so basically a flight attendant without a plane."

"That sounds amazing!" Josh beamed. Then he remembered the people squashed behind him. "Time to get snuggly in my pod...!"

"Enjoy your flight, sir." She smiled. "I predict a smooth journey today."

"Calm after the storm and all that!" Josh said with a grin as he headed through the curtain to first class.

He found his pod and stretched out, amusing himself looking at the menu. Guy would be back on the island by now, and Josh pictured him on the veranda with a pot of tea. If only he could've stayed there with him.

This is going to be the longest week ever.

Josh sighed and listened to the sounds of the airplane, the hum of engines and the polite chatter of his fellow passengers. He heard the doors close and looked out at Guadeloupe, shining in the sun. Somewhere out there, beyond the runways and the ocean, St Sebastian glittered. And he had left his heart on the island.

"Ladies and gentlemen, this is your captain speaking."

Not just any captain.

Josh dropped his glossy inflight magazine and stared at the speaker above his seat.

Guy. Guy is flying the plane.

"Welcome aboard this British Airways flight to London Heathrow. The forecast is excellent, we're right on schedule and I'd like to inform the gentleman sitting in seat A2 that a week was *far* too long to wait. Even a couple of hours was a stretch."

Josh blushed and turned with an awkward smile to his fellow passengers, but soon remembered that he couldn't see them cocooned in their pods.

"The marvelous Teri Norman will be looking after you today, and if she seems a little giddy, it's because she got engaged during her stopover on St Sebastian. A round of applause for Teri, if you'd be so kind."

And everyone obeyed with a polite clatter of applause, because when Guy requested *anything* in that smooth, merry voice, how could they not?

Teri, who's going to St Sebastian to live her dream.

"Teri and her team will take you through our safety procedures as we on the flight deck prepare for take-off. In nine hours we'll be landing in Blighty and I'll be eating cinnamon buns with the man I love. Until then, I can assure you that you're in *very* good hands. Cabin crew, please prepare for gate departure, we're raring to go."

Reluctantly, Josh buckled himself in. If only he could spend the next nine hours with Guy. But the same plane was enough — it was better than being on separate continents.

And soon they'd be home. *Together.*

Once the plane was in the air, Josh relaxed with a Buck's Fizz and chose a film to watch. He didn't pay much attention to it as a far more interesting film played out in his mind. The sun-drenched afternoon when he and Guy had swum off his private beach and made love on the sand afterward. And ended up in the bath.

Josh tucked himself under his blanket. The air con in the cabin was rather too enthusiastic. Yes, what a beautiful afternoon that had been, followed by a wonderful evening and a very romantic night.

Josh and his captain, falling asleep in each other's arms... Josh closed his eyes.

Some hours later he woke up, sure he'd imprinted his hand onto the side of his face. He yawned himself awake.

It was already dark.

Josh picked up his glass to finish his drink and he smiled as, underneath, he found a note.

I know this marvellous hotel near Heathrow... Perfect for poets and pilots. Love you, darling. Xxxxx

Josh grinned. He tore a sheet out of the notepad he'd bought at the airport with every intention of writing a poem. He hadn't, of course. But maybe he would one day. Josh scribbled his reply.

Do they serve cinnamon buns? Xxxx

He leaned forward in his seat and saw Teri talking to one of the other passengers. He waved to her. She trotted over and seconds later the note was on its way to Guy. A minute or so after that she was back, handing Josh his lover's reply.

Only with champagne. Xxxxx

Josh laughed.

Above him the speaker buzzed into life and Guy's voice filled the plane once more, as calm and cool as ever it was.

"Good evening, ladies and gentlemen, this is Captain Collingwood speaking. We're about to make our descent in London where the local time is eleven p.m.

I'm sorry to say that it's raining and rather chilly, with a temperature of nine degrees, so I hope you've packed a cuddly sweater. The seatbelt signs are now illuminated and we're clear for descent. Cabin crew, prepare for landing."

Josh sighed as he folded up his blanket. He wound his watch forward to eleven o'clock and brought his seat up, then fastened his belt. Nine degrees, when it had been thirty-three when they'd left Pointe-à-Pitre. He'd definitely be putting his jumper on when they landed, even though it hopefully wouldn't be too long before he'd be flinging it off.

But he was going to back to work on Monday. His tan would look good against his white shirt, but there was a team-building session to organize for the new on-road sales team, and handouts to print, and there was some new system for arranging photocopying, and—

I wish I was in St Sebastian.

He could be. There was no reason on Earth why not.

The rain rattled against the window but Josh saw only sunshine, thinking of himself and Guy, together on their island paradise. It wasn't a dream—it could be their reality. He had only to throw aside the sensible Josh Robertson who was forever blocking his way to fun and adventure—and grasp it.

"Ladies and gentlemen," Guy said as the plane came to a halt on the tarmac, "welcome to London Heathrow. On behalf of this British Airways crew, it's been a pleasure to fly with you today and I hope you have a very good evening—whatever you may be doing."

No one was going to be looking, so Josh blew a kiss at the speaker above his head. "I certainly know what *we're* going to be doing," Josh said.

He was spirited from the plane, through passport control, and collected his luggage. Josh had switched his phone on but he wasn't expecting to hear from Guy at once. The man had just safely landed a plane in a downpour after a nine-hour flight and presumably had more to do than send him saucy texts.

As he wheeled his case out of Arrivals, Josh looked up and saw his name. It was written in neat capitals on a piece of white paper, held in the manicured hand of a smiling BA employee.

"Mr. Robertson? Captain Collingwood has asked me to escort you through the terminal." She beamed brightly, despite the rain. "Did you have a pleasant trip?"

"I slept for most of it, but then, Captain Collingwood is an expert pilot!" Josh thought of those wonderful hands running over his body and a delicious shiver ran through him. *Expert in a lot of things.*

"He's certainly one of the prides of the fleet." His comrade smiled, her heels clicking efficiently through the enormous hall. Josh wondered where they were going, but wherever it was, it led to Guy, so that could only be a good thing.

A coffee shop.

And not just a coffee shop, but a branch of the same shop in which they had met just a week earlier.

"Captain Collingwood will be along as soon as he's completed his post-flight business." She escorted him to a table, where a latte and cinnamon bun already waited. "I've popped my card on the table. If you need anything at all, just call."

"Thanks!" Josh took his seat and sipped at his coffee. He took out his phone and snapped a selfie of himself biting into the bun. *Hope one's left for you xxxx*, and he sent it to Guy.

The reply took a moment.

Not if I know you! Xxxxx

Josh wiped his hands on his napkin and replied, *My lips are covered in sugar now. Will you kiss it off? Xxx*

Just as he pressed send, he noticed a disruption in the constant stream of passengers. A hen party returning from who-knew-where were cackling en masse, pointing farther along the concourse. Josh couldn't resist having a peep himself.

He should've guessed.

It was Guy. In full, glorious uniform, striding with easy confidence over the polished floor of the airport. Josh fell in love with him all over again. He was the most gorgeous man he'd ever seen, in and out of uniform. And Josh would've still thought so even if Guy drove a bus and lived in a terrace.

But that uniform…

Before Josh could stop himself, he was out of his seat, his trainers squeaking over the floor as he ran toward Guy.

And Guy quickened his pace into a run to meet Josh, the rest of the world falling away. As the hen party gave a whoop of delighted *awwwws*, Josh felt Guy's arms around his waist, then his feet were clear of the ground with the force of his lover's embrace.

Josh kissed him on the lips, leaving a trail of sugar. In a rush, he said, "Take me back to St Seb with you!"

"Every time, darling." Guy settled his cap on Josh's head. "How does Christmas in the Caribbean sound?"

"*Amazing!*" Josh grinned and tugged the hat to sit at an angle. "But let's make a go of it — what do you think? You could fly Victor's planes between the islands, and I can sort out the business stuff, and I promise never to tell you to be *solution focused, not problem focused*. We can have cinnamon buns for breakfast every day and throw parties every week!"

"You don't mean that, you've just got the Heathrow blues." His lover laughed, snuggling him close. "I love you, Josh, whether we're in the rain or the sun. You don't have to give anything up for me!"

Josh rested his head on Guy's shoulder and breathed in his scent. Masculine, spicy. Exciting. "I want to, though. Then we can be with each other all the time. And maybe drive each other up the wall, but at least we can go for a nice swim whenever we want!"

"How can I say no to that?" Guy kissed his cheek, still holding him tight. "Let's talk about it over champagne. In bed?"

"Yes," Josh decided. "In bed."

What the heck was in that bun?

Chapter Sixteen

It was another lovely day on St Sebastian. The clear blue sea was calm, and the breeze gently stirred the palms. Out on the beach, an arch of flowers framed Pierre, who was waiting for the grooms with Rey. There on the sand, perched in the neatly arranged seats, were their friends and family, some from England, some from St Seb's, the place that they now called home. Pris, Josh noted, was beaming almost as brightly as his own parents were, snapping photos on her mobile of the guests, whom she was martialing like a sergeant major. Teri looked on indulgently, taking plenty of photos of her own. And there, in the comfiest chair of all, his wife at his side, was Victor, the happiest retiree in Guadeloupe, happy in the knowledge that his business had passed into the safest hands he could hope for. Because who could be more passionate and sensible than the combined forces of *Gosh*?

Dressed in a dapper white linen suit, Josh wandered barefoot onto the beach, carrying a posy of rich orange flowers. He glanced up as his future husband approached.

And all over again, he was speechless.

It wasn't the uniform, but *the* uniform. *Wing Commander Collingwood*, as once he had been.

Guy met Josh's gaze and winked.

He can still surprise me, even after a year in his arms.

Josh took his captain's hand as they met at the end of the aisle and walked onward together to their future.

Want to see more from these authors? Here's a taster for you to enjoy!

The Captain's Flirty Fireworks
Catherine Curzon & Eleanor Harkstead

Excerpt

When Rob Monteagle pushed open the door of the King's Head, he walked into a lull in the conversation. He'd only recently moved to Longley Magna, and it seemed that the locals of the South Downs village were still getting the measure of him.

Rob nodded and gave a small wave to the other drinkers, and once they seemed satisfied that they knew who he was—a rather loud stage whisper from someone in the pub of "He's that new fireman!" helped—they went back to their Saturday night conversations.

He ordered a pint of the local ale and leaned back against the old bar, wondering how to strike up a conversation—wondering who would *want* him to. Everyone seemed settled in their own little groups, and when Rob had attempted to join in on his last visit to the pub, he'd received a jovial barrage of remarks about helmets and hoses. Still, he had to try.

Before Rob had a chance to move, the pub door swung open, admitting a blast of cold November air to the busy taproom. It admitted a man too, and the very sight of him sent a frisson through Rob just as it did every time he caught a glimpse of the stranger, who was usually to be seen on horseback.

Tonight, though, he was on his own two feet and his handsome face was lit by a smile brighter than any fire. He stood just inside the pub doorway and called to the assembled drinkers, "I need a hero who doesn't mind heights, at the double!"

Rob put his pint down on the bar. Now here was an opportunity to be useful to the community and — well, he had to be honest, the bloke was gorgeous.

"I don't know about a hero, but I'm not scared of heights. Been up a fair few ladders in my time!" He crossed the room and smiled into the man's sparkling dark eyes. "I'm Rob, the new fire officer at Longley Magna station — don't think we've been introduced."

"Ollie, and you look *just* like the hero I need," the man told him. He took Rob's hand and shook it, the dark green waxed jacket he wore rustling as he did. And jodhpurs, Rob noticed, though he tried hard not to. Why did this handsome man named Ollie *always* have to be in jodhpurs? "Terrified of heights, but always trying to save a damsel in distress — even if she *does* have a tail and whiskers!"

"Is it Smudge again?" the landlord called. Ollie's nod elicited a chorus of long-suffering groans from the drinkers. Then, still holding Rob's hand, he towed him out into the late afternoon dusk.

"There." Ollie pointed to the oak in the middle of the village green, where a black and white cat was sitting quite contentedly among the boughs. At the foot of the tree was an elderly woman, a dish in her hands that was clearly intended to tempt the creature down. "Can you hop up the tree and do the necessary for Mrs. Cooper's pride and joy?"

"Don't see why not!" Rob grinned.

Easy-peasy.

The old tree was a breeze to climb, with several low branches and thick bark that gave Rob purchase as he nimbly ascended the trunk. Once he was level with the cat, he sat astride the branch she had settled on and beckoned her.

"Smudge? Hey there, madam. Would you mind climbing down now?"

"Be careful!" Ollie called from where he had joined the lady with the dish. At the pub door drinkers gathered, watching the new firefighter save the day. The cat, meanwhile, began edging along the branch until she reached Rob. Then she nuzzled against him and let out a long, low purr.

Rob waved down to his audience. "We're okay!" He stroked Smudge, whispering assurances to her before slipping her into one of the large pockets of his peacoat. He made his way down carefully but jumped the last few feet and produced Smudge from his pocket, like a magician producing a rabbit from a hat. A cheer went up from the assembled drinkers as the cat nuzzled against his chin.

The lady took the cat in her arms despite the dish, snuggling her close as she told Rob, "Thank you! She does this every time I won't give her a sausage — she's a terror!"

Rob grinned. "We all like a sausage!"

"Some of us more than others." Ollie laughed. He patted Rob's shoulder and asked, "Buy you a beer to say thanks?"

"You don't have to do that, really, I'm happy to help." Rob was still grinning. "But go on then, I won't say no! Back to the King's Head?"

Which, Rob realized, was a daft question, because as far as he was aware, it was Longley Magna's only pub. And he had left a pint on the bar, and he couldn't really have two since he was on bucket duty in an hour, but despite all of that, he wasn't going to say no to the handsome man in the form-fitting jodhpurs.

"What're you drinking?" Ollie shepherded him through the drinkers who were on their way back into the pub, where the fire roared and the conversation hummed. He knew them all, Rob could see, with his companion receiving slaps on the back and cheery welcomes from what seemed like everyone. "Something fit for a hero?"

Awkward, Rob shook his head. "No, I'm not a hero — just a reckless fool with no fear of heights!"

He picked up his pint and was dismayed to see the spectacle of a pork scratching bobbing on the surface of his ale. "Wouldn't mind a new one of these, Ollie, if there's one going? A pint of the local ale *without* the garnish, please."

"One each of those, please, I've earned it today. Really put the saddle hours in!" Ollie beamed, slapping his hand down on the polished surface of the bar. "And a roast beef roll for me. Rob, anything to eat?"

"Bag of crisps would be nice." *Saddle hours?* Rob took in the jodhpurs again, and once more had to force himself to look somewhere else. Ollie's face seemed like a safe bet, but it made him even more aware of how attractive the man was. "So you often go riding, do you?"

"How else could he strut about in jodhpurs all day, every day?" The young woman behind the bar gave Ollie a cheeky wink before she pulled the pints. "What flavor're you after? We've got all the boring ones."

"You ride *every* day?" Rob stared open-mouthed at Ollie. "Do you run a riding school or—oh, sorry." He tried a winning smile at the woman who was serving them. "Boring old ready salted is fine, thanks."

"How many riding schools is it you've got now, Ollie?" She asked the question innocently enough, though Rob wondered if it was something that he was just *expected* to know. Village life could be like that, after all. "Is it more or less than you've got gold medals?"

"*Definitely* more riding schools than gold medals." Ollie laughed and passed over a handful of coins. He waved away the change and picked up his pint. "Shall we get a table?"

"Yeah, a table would be nice." *And no jokes about helmets or hoses. Yet.* "How did you win your medals, Ollie? I've got a one kilometer swimming badge, but I don't think I've ever met someone who's won a gold medal."

"Showjumping, in which I have occasional flashes of competence. They even made me captain of the team," Ollie told him, leading Rob toward an empty table beside the hearth. Here he put down his pint and unzipped the waxed jacket to reveal a crisp dark blue shirt tucked into the—*Don't look at the jodhpurs.* "I'm surprised to find a fireman who's *not* at work on Bonfire Night, and I'm trying terribly hard not to make any childish jokes about poles and hoses."

"It was either come out for a drink or stay at home and polish my helmet." Rob grinned and raised an eyebrow. At least that was one terrible joke out of the way. "I'm off duty, Captain Ollie, but I've got to scarper in a bit and shake my bucket around to raise some cash for charity."

"I'll think of you while I'm noshing on hot dogs and waving my sparkler around." Ollie laughed. "We're having a bit of a firework display at home, barbecue and all that business. Shame you've got a gig, you would've been more than welcome to be my plus one since my plus one is now very definitely a minus!"

"You're better off without him." The barmaid sniffed as she put down a plate in front of Ollie on which was an enormous bread roll stuffed with roast beef. Steam and the aroma of Sunday dinners rose from it, and Ollie gave a flamboyant rub of his hands. The barmaid leaned down to speak to Rob as though imparting a great secret. "We all said good riddance in here—he was a total *arse*."

"Sorry to hear that, Ollie." Rob tore into his bag of crisps. He didn't feel quite as bad now that his gaze kept traveling up and down Ollie's firm legs. His gaydar was still functioning. *What a relief.* "I split up with my boyfriend a few months ago, and ditto, *total arse.*"

"Well, there you go!" The barmaid laughed as she began to walk away, then called, "You look cute together to me! A captain and a fireman, I know a lot of girls who'd like that!"

"So does that mean I'm *finally* not the only gay in this particular village?" Ollie laughed and asked, "Do you want to share my beef?"

"You've certainly got plenty of beef there, Ollie! If you want to share, then I won't say no." Rob licked the salt from the crisps off his fingertips. "You are indeed no longer the only gay in Longley Magna."

"So, dig in and tell me all about your charity do. Lots of that goes on around here, usually arranged by flirty ladies of a certain age or old majors who like to have someone to bark at." He cut the roll in half and edged Rob's share across the plate. "Which are you stuck with tonight?"

Rob nodded his thanks and helped himself to his half of the roll. "Some posh pillock in a big house who loves nothing better than bossing everyone around. I've spent the past month doing my best to help him — bloody hell, he'd try the patience of a saint!"

He bit into the roll and tried to hide his surprise at just how good it was. Longley Magna, it seemed, wasn't the sort of village to dish up dry, tough old fare.

Ollie crossed his long legs at the ankle, his polished leather boots reflecting the firelight that glowed in the grate.

"Well, on behalf of the village, I apologize. We do have some right old miseries in these parts. Has he been terribly difficult?"

"We've all been laughing about it down the station." Rob wagged his roll at Ollie as he did his best to reproduce the plummy bray of his nemesis. *"Risk assessment*, he said, *I've got no need of a bally risk assessment! You didn't see Wellington filling out a risk assessment!* I did try to explain that the fire brigade and the Army are rather different, and that going into battle in 1815 isn't quite the same as launching fireworks into the air above a village two hundred years later, but he wasn't having it, and spoke at me as if I hadn't the foggiest about fire safety. *We've got buckets of sand on standby, Sonny Jim!* He *really* did call me Sonny Jim — what a prat."

Ollie threw his head back and laughed, a booming, upper-class sound that perfectly suited the sort of man who performed mercy dashes while wearing a waxed jacket and polished riding boots. Then he joined Rob with a *slightly* posher version of his own voice and said, "Now look here, sonny, when Pa landed his Spit on the croquet lawn just in time for tea, we didn't fill in *forms*. Did Churchill fill in forms, Sonny Jim? Did he? Eh?"

"Oh, God, that's him to a T!" Rob sighed. "And there was me thinking I was heading for a quiet life when I moved here. I didn't reckon with bossy toffs."

"Well, speaking as a fairly easy-going toff, I *might* be back here after the party breaks up." Ollie took a sip from his glass and met Rob's gaze. "Just so you know, in case you've got nothing planned after you put your bucket away."

Rob put the remains of the roll on the plate. If he wasn't imagining things, Ollie's invitation was a sort-of-date. Did Rob want to go there, after what had happened with—no, he wouldn't spare his ex a moment's thought. He'd come to Longley Magna for a new start, and if that meant drinking ale with a hot man in tight jodhpurs, then so be it.

"As a matter of fact, I didn't have anything planned. But I do *now*. So thank you."

"How the hell have I not seen you around the village?" Ollie asked. "When did you move in?"

"Couple of months ago. My old aunt died back in the spring and left me her cottage. So when I've not been at work, I've been sprucing the place up. I have tried to mingle with the locals, but..." Rob met Ollie's gaze again. "I think I've seen you about—heard hooves outside on the road and saw—" *A magnificent figure on horseback.* "A bloke on a horse."

"That'd be me!" Ollie beamed, though when he spoke again his voice was more measured. "People around here are a pretty friendly bunch but you know how villages can be. How are you settling in, apart from miserable old duffers and their charity buckets? Are the Magnans making you welcome?"

"I don't know the first thing about horses, but you look pretty impressive in the saddle to me." Rob grinned, hoping that Ollie must've realized by now that he wasn't indifferent to him. "The team up at the fire station are great, and the post office that doubles as a supermarket and general supplier of random things is amazing. Haven't had much time to mingle, though. I was hoping this evening I might get to meet the locals — and I have. I've met *you*."

Rob raised his pint to Ollie. Ollie raised his and clinked it against Rob's.

"God bless Bonfire Night — it has its uses!"

Rob shone what he hoped was his cheekiest smile. "There might even be fireworks before the night's through, Captain."

"You *are* the village hero." Ollie innocently popped the tip of his finger between his lips as he finished eating. "The only question is, do I change for our drink tonight or keep the joddies on?"

Rob ran his hand through his short, neat hair. So Ollie had noticed the direction of Rob's glance. *It's not as if he could've missed it.* His voice huskier than he had intended, Rob replied, "I think you should leave them on. For our drink, at least."

Should he be flirting so outrageously like this with a man he'd only just met — even if he had seen him riding about the lanes, that tempting, firm bottom rising up and down in the saddle? If this all went arse over tit, Rob would be trapped in a village with a gorgeous but failed one-night stand.

"I'll leave them on for the drink," Ollie promised, his dark eyes sparkling. "And we can see where we go from there."

Hot need shot to Rob's groin and he tried to shift in his chair to disguise it. He wanted Ollie with a desire he hadn't known for a long time. How tempting to pull him into his arms now and kiss him, and feel that magnificent arse under his hands. How he'd love to make Ollie grip the headboard of the bed and —

"Is that the time?" Rob pushed up his sleeve and looked at his watch. "Sorry, Ollie, I've got to go. But I'll see you back here later. Nine? Nine-thirty-ish?"

"I'll be here by half past," Ollie told him. "Boots polished for the occasion, Officer — or whatever I should call a fireman when I'm not making jokes about poles."

"Station Manager Monteagle." Rob clasped Ollie's hand and drew close enough to whisper, "Just so you know, when you're riding, your backside is…perfect."

"When you were climbing that tree in those jeans," Ollie whispered in reply, "I forgot what day it was."

Rob didn't move away. Whatever cologne Ollie was wearing, Rob was determined to memorize it so he could think of it while he stood about in the cold and dark, shaking a bucket for pennies.

"Half-nine, then." Rob let his lips just brush against Ollie's skin as he let go of his hand. Did Ollie tremble, or was it Rob?

Perhaps it was both of them.

"See you then." Ollie winked one mischievous eye. "Sonny Jim."

Rob laughed. As he left, more reluctantly than he wanted to admit, he waved Ollie goodbye.

PUBLISHING

Sign up for our newsletter and find out about all our romance book releases, eBook sales and promotions, sneak peeks and FREE romance books!

About the Authors

Catherine Curzon

Catherine Curzon is a royal historian who writes on all matters of 18th century. Her work has been featured on many platforms and Catherine has also spoken at various venues including the Royal Pavilion, Brighton, and Dr Johnson's House.

Catherine holds a Master's degree in Film and when not dodging the furies of the guillotine, writes fiction set deep in the underbelly of Georgian London.

She lives in Yorkshire atop a ludicrously steep hill.

Eleanor Harkstead

Eleanor Harkstead often dashes about in nineteenth-century costume, in bonnet or cravat as the mood takes her. She can occasionally be found wandering old graveyards, and is especially fond of the ones in Edinburgh. Eleanor is very fond of chocolate, wine, tweed waistcoats and nice pens. She has a large collection of vintage hats, and once played guitar in a band. Originally from the south-east, Eleanor now lives somewhere in the Midlands with a large ginger cat who resembles a Viking.

Catherine and Eleanor love to hear from readers. You can find their contact information, website and author biographies at https://www.pride-publishing.com.

www.ingramcontent.com/pod-product-compliance
Lightning Source LLC
Chambersburg PA
CBHW020423180626
46812CB00003B/1122